THE
HOME PLACE

THE
HOME PLACE

by *DOROTHY THOMAS*

Illustrated by Ruth Gannett

UNIVERSITY OF NEBRASKA PRESS · LINCOLN

First Bison Book printing October, 1966

Second Bison Book printing April, 1967

Bison Book edition published by arrangement with Alfred A. Knopf, Inc.

for

MY MOTHER

CONTENTS

THE
HOME PLACE

FALL : WAKING before she was
aware of Ralph's heavy breathing and the warmth
of his body beside her, Phyllis thought first that she
was in her own blue bed in her father's house, and
then that she was in the big maple bed in the house
that Ralph had built for her when everything was
fine. Heavily reality came over her like the "billows
down over the soul" her mother-in-law was always
singing about. She opened her eyes and saw the
eight gray squares that made the windows in the
winter dawn and knew that she was in the old four-
poster bed in Grandma Young's room in the little

3

house on the Young home place.

Overhead, in Edna and Tom's room, the alarm stopped its muffled whirring and she heard the thud of a window being let down; Tom was up and Edna would be up and on the stairs in a minute, stumping down in her stocking-feet to dress by the heater in the dining-room.

Phyllis put a hand on her husband's shoulder and began giving him gentle shoves, saying in a sharp whisper: "Ralph! Ralph!"

He drew away and mumbled: "Whata you want?"

"Get up," Phyllis whispered, "the alarm's gone off. Tom's up."

"Oh, Lord," Ralph moaned, and with an elbow drew the covers well over his head. Phyllis kept at him until he woke and sat up. He swayed backward and forward, his hands hanging limply over his parted knees. "What time is it?" he asked.

"I don't know," Phyllis said. "You won't drop off if I get up to see?"

"No, I'm awake. Seems like I haven't been asleep."

Phyllis slid from the bed and felt with her toes for her mules and when she found them went with her hands out before her, feeling her way toward

4

the middle of the room and reached up to turn on the light.

Ralph heard the click of the light-chain against the bulb and laughed shortly. "How many times you going to try to turn on that dead light?"

"No telling," Phyllis said; "I can't get used to their being off." She was at the far side of the room cautiously moving a chair.

"What you doing over there," Ralph wanted to know; "isn't the light on the dresser?"

"Be still," Phyllis whispered, and a moment later he heard her fumbling among the things on the dresser for the little gilt slipper that held the matches. She struck the match twice, leaving long phosphorescent streaks on the sandpaper cat match-scratcher before she got a light. She turned the wick low. "I was fixing a coat so the light wouldn't shine in Betty's eyes," she said.

Ralph got stiffly out of bed and went shivering across the room to put down the window. Then he came and stood behind Phyllis—she was beginning to comb her hair—and picked up his watch from the dresser and squinted at it. "Quartera five! Good God!" he said.

Phyllis was drawing the comb rapidly through her long black hair. "Betty fretted so," she said; "I was up with her a dozen times, couldn't keep her covered."

"So?" Ralph said. "Didn't hear you." He was getting into his clothes and burring his lips noisily.

"I tried to be quiet. You were restless too, kept groaning."

"I was dead."

Phyllis was coiling her hair, frowning into the dim and speckled looking-glass. "Ralph, I'm going to say something," she said. "I can't stand it any longer!"

"Huh? About the boys?"

Phyllis drew the combings from the comb, wound them about her finger, held them gingerly between her fingertips a second, then stuffed them into the china hair-receiver, whirled about, and put her hands behind her, gripping the edge of the dresser. "Yes, I am," she said, "and I don't care if it brings the roof down. We've as much right to this house, to peace in this house, as Edna and Tom have. The boys tease and tease Betty until she cries in her sleep: 'Don't, George! Quit, Tommy!' There's no sense in boys their size picking on a little thing like Betty. They keep her scared and cross all the time. She was never like that at home. You know she wasn't!"

6

Ralph was wrestling with a broken suspender-buckle. "Better go easy," he said. "Edna's so sour now she don't even look at me. Never says a word."

"Then you talk to Tom!"

Ralph sat down on the bed and stamped a foot into a shoe and tied it before he answered her. "Ya, and have him blow a fuse," he said. "I've got to work with that sorehead all day, and that's no cinch."

"All right, then, I talk to Edna," she said, and turned away from him, her teeth on her under lip.

Ralph slid his watch into his overall pocket and went across the room and looked down at his little daughter where she lay on old Grandma Young's sofa. Even in sleep her little fists were doubled up tightly, and her face, white against her brown curls, was tense. "Sure she's comfortable?" he asked his wife. "If this old sofa's as hard as it was when I used to get sat down on it, when I was a kid, it's hard."

"There's the down comfort under her."

"Tell you what," Ralph said; "if she complains they bother her today, I'll talk to Tom. But let's not get things stirred up again if we can help it."

Phyllis sighed and looked quickly into his eyes as though she would say she was sorry to have plagued him with any trouble in the world. She took hold of

7

his hands and lifted them, palms upward, and turned him to the light. "How're your wrists?" she asked.

"Oh, sore."

"Bad as yesterday? Didn't the liniment help any?"

"I don't know. They're stiff."

Phyllis took his hands and pressed the wrists gently against her cheeks. "Well, well," she said softly, "got me a big old, stiff old corn-picker!" Ralph clasped his hands behind her neck and drew her head against him. "Stiff, all right," he said; "can't begin to pick with Tom. Never could, even when I was home." He spoke as though home were some other place.

"You're not used to it, that's all," Phyllis said. "You'll catch up. We'd better get out there." She drew away from him, and he put out his hand to open the door for her, but the door swung open before his hand touched the knob, and his little old grandmother gaped up at him with her head atremble.

"Young man, what are you doing in my room?" she piped, clasping her hands over her little round stomach and straightening up as well as she could.

"Oh, dear," Phyllis sighed, and struck her hands together with a hopeless little pop.

8

"Hello, Gran'ma!" Ralph bawled, cupping his hands close to the old woman's ear; "you know *me*. I'm Ralph! You gave us your room, don't you know? Your bed's in the kitchen."

"Oh," old Grandma Young said, "that's right. I forgot, I guess. Acourse. But who's this woman?" She drew back, tucking down her chin and wrinkling her old forehead and scowling at Phyllis.

Ralph laughed, put his hand on his wife's shoulder, and pushed her toward his grandmother. "Phyllis, my wife!" he yelled.

The old woman grinned foolishly and spatted at him with a quavery hand. "Don't try to fox me," she said; "you! Your wife! She isn't any such thing. You ain't big enough to get married. Is my bed ready?"

"Now, Gran'ma, your bed's out in the kitchen," Ralph said.

"Go on, 'tis not," the old woman said, still playfully. She ducked under his arm and tottered across the room, then made a feeble attempt to lift her bony old leg up on the bed. Ralph came and picked her up, put her in the bed, and tucked the covers up under her chin. "There! Go to sleep!" he yelled.

Phyllis was quieting Betty. Ralph blew out the light and motioned for Phyllis to go ahead of him.

9

He gave her a husbandly spank as she went through the door.

"Oh, why'd you let her get in bed?" she asked.

"Why not?" Ralph said. "Can't let her stand in the cold all morning and argue."

Phyllis stopped to spread the covers over little Tommy's bare legs. Edna's boys slept on the folding couch in the dining-room. "Edna'll have everything done," she said.

"Well, let her. Get up this time of morning—like we had a crop to pick!"

In the kitchen there was already a good warmth and the smell of burning cobs and hot grease and coffee. Edna stood at the stove, a crock of pancake batter in one hand and a case-knife in the other. She scorned the pancake-turner Phyllis had brought from her home. She did not turn or speak.

"Tom and Papa out at the barn?" Ralph asked cheerfully.

"Acourse," Edna said.

Ralph and Phyllis exchanged mock sour looks; Ralph got his sheepskin from behind the kitchen door and went out. Phyllis, left alone with Edna, took a loaf of bread from the tin box and began cutting slices. Edna turned from the stove to say:

10

"That's enough. We got cakes." Phyllis put the bread on the table and looked about for something else to do.

"Ain't your girl going to school today?" asked Edna.

"Yes."

"Then hadn't you better be putting up her lunch?"

Phyllis looked at her sister-in-law's broad back, her rising anger nauseating her a little. She had learned to wait about putting up Betty's school lunch until Edna was out seeing to her chickens. She knew it irritated Edna to see her putting the thermos bottle full of chocolate or soup and an orange or apple into the child's pail. Edna's boys thrived on thick sausage sandwiches and cold mince-meat pie. Phyllis set the butter in the warming oven to get it soft enough for spreading sandwiches.

It was a relief when Mamma Young came in with little Betty in her arms. She had wrapped the child in a blanket and was hugging and kissing her, making quite a fuss over her. "There, there," she was crooning, "was Gran'ma's girl scared? Was her scared of old Gran'ma snoring?" She opened the oven door, pulled a chair toward the stove, and sat down with

11

the child on her lap. She held the little feet toward the oven's warmth, her sturdy pink hands clasping the ankles. She paid no attention to Edna's angry shove of the pancake griddle to the far side of the stove. Phyllis, watching, saw that Mamma Young was not going to let her eldest boy's wife's sulks faze her. The old woman put a hand on the child's forehead. "Phyllis," she said, "this child's caught cold. I believe she's got a fever."

"I don't know how I'm to tell," Phyllis said; "I've no thermometer, you know."

Edna turned and looked at Phyllis, her small blue eyes bright and belligerent. One of her boys had broken Phyllis's thermometer playing doctor, and Edna had not offered to replace it with a new one. Neither of the women had forgotten.

"Well, I don't need a thermometer to tell when a child's feverish," Mamma Young said. "Look at the fire in her cheeks, and how dry her lips are. Don't feel a bit good, do you, Sweet?"

Betty laid her head against her grandmother's soft bosom and sighed a whimpering sigh. Mamma Young carried her to old Grandma Young's bed in the kitchen corner and covered and patted her. "You sleep awhile longer," she said. Then she went in the pantry, came out with a glass of jelly in one hand and a jar of jam in the other, and went to the table with them.

Phyllis, watching her, liked the soft roll of her mother-in-law's walk. There was something at once soft and strong about it. The old lady was smiling to herself. "Arch's mother's in Phyllis's bed," she said to Edna, ignoring that young woman's gloom. "I heard her runtin' around in there and Betty acrying. Seems like Old Gran'ma can't get used to sleepin' out here in the kitchen, even if it was her own idea. One day she understands it clear enough and next day she's all mixed up and wants back in there. Don't know where she's at or anything. Thinks Ralph and Phyllis are strangers and don't belong here."

A loud breath that was almost a snort came from Edna's direction, and Phyllis thought that Edna might as well have said: "Isn't the old lady right?"

"Ain't it time you got your boys up, Edna?" Mamma Young asked.

"I'll get 'em up," Edna said. "Mind the cakes, will you?" This last to her mother-in-law. Edna seldom asked Phyllis to do anything, but if she saw her empty-handed her very back showed her disapproval. She went into the dining-room to wake her boys, slamming the door. Alone in the kitchen,

Phyllis and her mother-in-law smiled at each other. There had never been anything but good feeling between them in the three weeks Phyllis and Ralph had been in the house. Whether Mamma Young liked her just because she liked her or because she had borne her her only granddaughter, Phyllis did not know, but she was very glad of her goodwill.

The men were heard on the porch, and Mamma Young said: "Put the butter'n syrup on, will you, Phyllis?" Phyllis, when the old woman moved in her path, put an arm about her plump shoulders and gave her a squeeze, being careful not to tip the syrup-pitcher.

The three men came in, dipped water from the range reservoir to the wash-pan, and washed in turn, Tom first. "Ah-ah," Grandpa Young groaned loudly, his face in the roller towel, just as he always did. Phyllis watched first Tom, then her husband, scrutch down to see into the little looking-glass to comb their hair.

She wondered why the glass had never been hung higher on the wall. "Why haven't you hung the glass higher?" she asked Grandpa, and was surprised to find herself speaking her thought aloud.

Grandpa Young laughed. "Hung for Harvey," he said, with the fondness in his tone that the

14

Youngs dropped into when they spoke of Harvey, their baby. "Yes, sir, brought that mirror home about the time Harvey put on long pants and begun to spruce up to spark the Drier girl, didn't I, Mamma?"

" 'Bout, I guess. Only you got your boys mixed, Papa. It was Tom here liked the Drier girl." Mamma Young seemed a little embarrassed making this correction and smoothed a kind hand down her eldest son's arm and smiled without looking into his eyes.

Edna came in in time to hear her say: "—liked the Drier girl," and looked angrily at her mother-in-law and suspiciously at her husband. Phyllis had not before heard any of them speak of the Drier girl, yet she felt the name's importance. Papa whistled thinly as he combed his hair. It was plain he realized he had said something he should not have said. Edna's boys had come in and were making a great racket. The middle one, George, had on only one shoe and was running limpingly around the table with the other two boys after him. Edna held the shoe in her hand. "Will you fix this, Papa?" she asked; "the sole's loose."

"Sure will, sure will," Papa said, "soon as I've had my breakfast. Breakfast ready, Mamma?"

"Yes, Arch," his wife said; "it's up and on the

15

table. Come on."

Edna was seeing to her boys' washing and combing.

"You kids pipe down," Tom said with very little spirit when he saw them scuffling over the towel. Phyllis felt that his half-hearted efforts at discipline were mainly for her benefit. He really did not mind their din and got cross with them only when they fought or when they disobeyed him out and out.

"Where's Betty?" little George yelled; "ain't she coming to the table?"

"She's sleeping in old Gran'ma's bed; don't wake her," his grandmother admonished, and put a hand on his shoulder and pushed him toward the breakfast table. "Your Gran'pa's waiting on you," she said.

Tommy, the oldest boy, ran to the bed to look at his sleeping cousin, and his grandma said: "Come on away from her!"

"He's not touchin' her!" Edna said sourly. Grandma got them all quiet at the table at last, after much chair-scraping and some scuffling among the boys, and when all the heads were bowed Grandpa said in a voice an octave lower than his speaking voice: "Our Father, we thank Thee for this Thy hand's bounty. Bless this food to our use and us to

Thy service. Forgive us our sins. Care for our loved ones and lead us in the paths of righteousness. Amen." The plates were turned over and Edna got up from her chair and brought the crockful of cakes from the warming oven, then took her place at the stove to fry more cakes and have them ready. They ate without talking.

"Let me fry awhile," Phyllis offered when she had eaten her cake.

Edna did not answer for the space of time it took her to turn the three cakes on the griddle. Then: "Better get your girl up, hadn't you?"

"No, I'll let her sleep to the last minute."

"That's right," Mamma Young said.

"Betty sick?" Tom asked.

"Didn't sleep well," Ralph said.

"Likely ate too many biscuits last night," Edna said.

"She didn't have biscuits," Phyllis said, trying to keep her rising irritation out of her voice. "I don't give her hot biscuits for supper."

"That's right," Edna said. "Got your stomach, ain't she?"

"There's nothing wrong with my stomach or hers," Phyllis said.

Ralph looked at her warningly. "That's right,"

17

he said casually. "You can eat anything, can't you, Baby?"

"Baby, baby!" young Tommy crowed loudly, his mouth full of cake and syrup, and began to choke. His father struck him smartly between the shoulders; he swallowed, rubbed the tears from his eyes, and finished: "Uncle Ralph called you a *baby*, Aunt Phyllis!"

"Shut up," Tom said, "and watch what you're doing."

Phyllis got up from the table and went to get Betty, who had waked. Old Grandma Young came out of the dining-room, her hands held tremblingly before her, and announced from the doorway, standing in her nightgown and Phyllis's good coat: "There's a raw wind; it's agoin' to blizzard. Have you seen to the stock, Arch?"

Ralph got up and went to her, took Phyllis's coat from her shoulders, put her shawl around her, and yelled: "Want your breakfast, Gran'ma, or do you want to go back to bed?"

The old lady considered, puckering her lips and plucking Ralph's sleeve with her dry fingers. "I don't know," she said plaintively; "never slept a wink. I was worryin' about George the whole night."

18

"Dream about him?" Ralph shouted.

Phyllis wondered why Ralph cared to spend so much time humoring the old woman. He seemed to like especially to hear her "go on" about his Uncle George, who had run away to the Klondike and never been heard from. Ralph led his grandmother to her place at the long table and sat her down.

"Yes, I did," she said, much pleased, "but I can't remember it good. All that's clear is, he came in that door, with a bucketful of gold, a milkpail full, and I said: 'Georgie boy, what have you there in that pail?' and he said: 'Milk and honey, Ma,' and I looked, and sure enough, 'twas gold, pure molten gold." She said this last in a sad, dreamy voice and fingered the edge of the blue-veined oilcloth. She looked up and around at them. "Have you had the blessing without me?" she asked. "Guess so," and held up her plate with both hands, like a child, for the cakes her daughter-in-law brought.

Grandpa Young got up from the table and went to the cellarway, where, on a ledge, he kept his cobbling kit. He sat down near the kitchen window and adjusted the little shoe to the last, between his knees. While he was trimming the edge of the sole with his knife he put out his tongue and ran it slowly from one corner of his mouth to the other. Little George, behind his grandfather's chair, put out his tongue in a mocking gesture, and the other boys giggled. Phyllis wished for the right to slap them soundly. She remembered her patience of her school-teaching days and wondered why she could not keep from being annoyed.

"Well, let's get moving," Tom said, and got his sheepskin and cap from behind the door. "Let's have those mended gloves, Edna," he said. Edna brought the gloves and he took them from her absent-mindedly and without thanks.

Phyllis was laying Betty's place at the table with the blue and yellow Mother Goose plate and mug that had been a gift from her father to Betty. Ralph went to her, his cap under his arm, and kissed her. "Where's the girl?" he asked.

"Mother's combing her hair in the other room," Phyllis said. She was the only one to call Mamma Young "Mother."

Ralph took a step toward the dining-room door, and Tom cried, jerking his cap down over his forehead: "Oh, for Pete's sake, let's get going!" Ralph swung about and followed him.

Edna, putting cobs into the stove and frowning over the heat from the coals, said to no one in particular: "Be time to come in by the time they get

out to the field!" Phyllis wondered whether her bitterness was all for the time that was lost. She had never seen Tom kiss Edna or show her special attention of any kind.

Grandpa Young had finished with the shoe. "There you are, there you are," he said after he had felt carefully to see that there were no tacks to hurt the little foot, and handed the shoe to George. The boy took it silently and hopped to the bed to put it on.

Little Betty came in with her hand in her grand-mother's. She was dainty, with her hair nicely curled and the pink ruffles of her neatly ironed apron under her chin. Phyllis lifted her into her place, where a mug of milk, an orange, and a bowl of oatmeal were waiting for her, and tucked a napkin under her curls. The orange was a right but a shameful thing. Phyllis knew that even Mamma Young, much as she adored the child, thought oranges for every day, in the winter-time, a real extravagance. Even Ralph, she knew, thought that an orange for breakfast, with things the way they were, "pretty steep." Phyllis stood between the family and the orange, hoping nothing would be said. "Just the juice, please, Mother," Betty said; "I don't want to *eat* it." Phyllis felt tears come to her eyes. Her hand closed on Bet-

22

ty's little shoulder. "Eat it," she said sharply, and the child, alarmed, ate the orange, section by section.

Edna came to the breakfast table with her plate full of pancakes. She did not look at Betty, but Phyllis knew that she had seen the orange. Grandpa came and tapped Phyllis on the arm with a gnarled forefinger. "I'm going to town," he said; "if you don't mind Betty going early, I can take her."

"What's wrong with the boys riding?" Edna asked before Phyllis had time to answer. The old man raised both hands in an unconscious, soothing gesture. "Sure," he said, "all of them, sure," and to Phyllis: "If you don't mind. If the teacher ain't there yet, I'll see there's a good fire before I go."

"All right. That'll be nice," Phyllis said, and then saw with dread little Betty alone in the schoolhouse with her three ornery cousins.

"Here, here! Don't do that," Grandpa said, and Phyllis turned to see one of the boys down on all fours, chasing the other two with her good coat over his back, the corners and the sleeves dragging on the floor. She snatched it off him and went with it into her bedroom and came out with Betty's wraps.

Mamma Young was very dubious about letting Betty go to school at all. Old Grandma, canny as she always was when there was a word of sickness in the air, said: "It's a raw wind, the kinda wind to bring a child home with a rising in the head might cost her her hearing."

"I want to go," little Betty said; "I feel good now"; and Grandpa picked her up and smoothed his cheek against hers and said: "I'll keep her wrapped good," and carried her out to the wagon.

Phyllis stood at the window and watched them drive away, Betty in the high seat with her grandfather, the boys scuffling in the wagon-bed.

Edna went out to see to her chickens. Washing dishes with Mamma Young, Phyllis said: "I wish old Gran'ma could have her room back. She comes in almost every morning and thinks it's still hers."

"I know," Mamma Young said; "all she keeps her wits for, for sure, seems, is the weather and sickness."

"What about the room up in the ell?" Phyllis asked. "Isn't there room up there I could put all the stuff in one end and set up a bed in the other?" She asked this rather breathlessly, not wanting her mother-in-law to know how very much it meant to her to have the room. Mamma Young had been so nice about moving old Grandma and fixing the little bed for her in the kitchen.

"Why, Child, you'd freeze up there," Mamma

24

Young said. "There's no fire under, you know. We've never set up a stove in Arch's and my room. And there's no floor laid up there. Just boards laid across for the trunks and things to rest on. We were going to lay a floor up there once, even took the lumber up, but Tom and Arch's used a good half that floorin', I wager, for one thing and another. I don't know how many times they've come down carryin' a board or two for this and that. And the walls ain't plastered, you know—just the bare walls, not even lath. There's no light, acourse. We didn't wire in there, but it don't matter, acourse, until we can afford to run the light-plant again."

"I'd like to go up and look at it," Phyllis said.

"All right, all right; soon as we've set up the dishes."

They went up the narrow stairway, Mamma Young ahead, past Tom's and Edna's room to the ell-room door. With her fingers Phyllis turned the bent nail that held the knobless door closed and they went in. The front part of the room was pretty well filled with trunks, boxes, a discarded set of driving harness, broken chairs, and dismembered bedsteads. Onions and seed-corn hung from the rafters.

Phyllis stood with her shoulders hunched and

shivering, her hands in her armpits, and looked at the room through her breath. "There's enough flooring to floor half of it," she said; "more than half."

"Well, 'spect Arch would lay it for you, yes, I'm sure he would, first day he ain't workin'."

"I can do it myself; I can nail down boards," Phyllis said. "May I have it?"

"Why, bless your heart, Child, acourse you can have it, if you want it, but it'll be cold sleepin' up here."

"I've plenty of bedding. Are there nails enough?"

"Oh, I'm sure, of one kind and another. Let's get the oil stove up here if you're going to do it now. I'll help you clear the place."

Between them they carried up the big oil stove, and while the room was heating, Phyllis tidied old Grandma's bedroom and the dining-room. Edna watched her hunting nails in all possible places, but she asked no questions.

Phyllis found Mamma Young, her shawl about her, sorting boxes of stored-away stuff and filling a cob-basket with papers and rags to be burned. "I'll wear down this pile of junk," she said, "so's there'll be more room. Old magazines and letters and stuff the boys saved." She emptied a paper sack of old

26

photographs and snapshots into her lap and began sorting them, throwing some into the cob-basket. Phyllis cleared a place nearest the doorway, laid two boards, and felt happier than she had felt in months, when she nailed them down. Mamma Young was blowing on her hands to warm them and saying: "My, my," over picture after picture. "What fools women are when it comes to their hair," she said; "but a pretty girl, she's pretty still, no matter how she's fixed up."

"Have you found a pretty one?" Phyllis asked.

"Yes, the little Drier girl."

Phyllis got up from her knees and came to have a look. "Why, she's lovely," she said; "does she live around here?"

"Can you read the German under it?" Mamma Young asked. "I can't, but I remember what it says: 'You're a flower.'"

" '*Du bist wie eine Blume*,' " Phyllis read.

"Yes, that's right. Her father wrote it there. She oughta been Tom's wife, by rights. Woulda been, but Drier, he was pro-German, they said, and he moved down to that little German town, corner the state, I forgot its name—they've changed it since—and that winter got the flu, all of them, and it took her right off. I felt bad about it this morning, Papa

27

bringing her name up like that, gettin' things mixed and thinking it was Harvey was interested in her. Tom was such a youngster, why, he wasn't over seventeen. She was sixteen."

"And what about Edna?" Phyllis asked. They had gossiped very little, she and her mother-in-law. Her mother-in-law talked much, when she was not singing hymns, and her presence was always comforting and seemed to take away some of the chill of the trouble that had come on them, but they had not gossiped.

Mamma Young sighed. "Oh, he just started going with her—I don't know. A man starts going with a neighbor girl like that, and after a while, if there's been no trouble or anything, it's kinda hard to quit, not without a reason. After he'd been going with her about a year—for so long there he'd not gone with anybody and we thought he just didn't care for girls and never was going to get over that little Drier girl—why, he came in one day and said if Papa thought it was all right he'd put up a house across the road. Arch was willing—we had it then."

Phyllis took the picture of the little Drier girl in her hands and looked at it. "She was so fair," she said.

"Yes, very light-complected, with blue eyes. A
28

mighty nice girl." Mamma Young went on with her sorting and her Oh-mying as the pictures brought either amusement or sadness, and Phyllis laid flooring. She worked as fast she could, for she wanted, if possible, to have the room ready when Ralph came in at noon. Once she hit her thumb and rocked back and forth, the injured hand between her knees, her eyes blurred with tears, and did not say anything. Then she got up and went to the window and looked out across the rutted lead-gray road toward the house Tom built for Edna. Smoke came from the chimneys and eddied downward. Strangers lived there now. Tom's place had had to go, and because Tom and his father had "got Ralph started" and Ralph had failed and lost his "place" too, Edna hated Ralph and Phyllis, and Tom carried a scornful, silent grudge.

"Want to see Edna in her wedding dress?" Mamma Young asked.

"She looks a lot the same," Phyllis said. Somehow she had expected a wedding veil to make a different woman of Edna. "Her shoulders are so heavy."

"Yes, yes, they are. That comes from workin' in the fields. All those folks do, right along with the boys. She'd be out there pickin' corn now if Tom would let her. It takes the delicacy out of a girl, I

29

think. I never did a thing outside when I was a girl, and Arch has never asked it of me, except acourse if there were more cows fresh at once than he could milk. Old Gran'ma, she'd have liked me to do more gardening, I think; but my, the house and the babies are enough, seems to me, with the chickens and canning and all, for any woman. She used to grumble at me—but she's forgotten now, I guess; been with us so long she thinks now I'm hers—was born hers. Yes, sir, one day she said to me: 'That happened when you was a baby. Or was it before you was born?' she says. Yes, she's forgot altogether how she felt against Arch marryin' me.

Mamma Young went downstairs to help Edna peel vegetables for dinner, and when she came up again she leaned against the door and stood smiling. "She'd give her eyes to know," she said, "Edna would, what you're up to up here, but she didn't ask and I didn't tell her."

"I'm done!" Phyllis said. "Now will you help me set up the bed?" She chose the biggest of the bedsteads and they set it up. Phyllis had to saw two new slats from a remaining, badly warped piece of flooring. "I know well what went with those old slats," Mamma Young said, tenderly. "Little Harvey made 'em into stilts. He was the slightest child I had, and to think the size he is now! Six foot three! To think of him playin' football all four years and steppin' into such a good job. This mattress is a little old, but I guess you won't feel the lumps much when you get a couple of feather ticks over it."

Phyllis brought up bedding from her trunks in old Grandma's room, and they made the bed, Mamma Young exclaiming over the beauty of the blankets. "—and such good sheets, too; my, you'd think you meant to marry a city man when you filled your chest up. All those towels, too, you got."

Phyllis laughed. "I didn't have anybody in mind," she said, "until I got my school and met Ralph."

"I think it's nice," Mamma Young said. "He wrote home about meeting you, and he never wrote about girls when he was in school—not one those two years, though he had 'em, I guess; they all do."

They made a little bed for Betty of a folded feather bed in a great packing-box set on two chairs. They were done, all but sweeping up the sawdust, when they heard Tom and Ralph come in. Mamma went down for the broom and came up with two red and white quilts over her arm. "There!" she said, and took a ball of cord and a ring of safety-pins from her pocket. "Nail up nails and tie the cord

31

across and we'll hang the quilts for curtains to shut off the junk end of the room.

"Stay out! Stay out!" the old woman called excitedly to Ralph when she heard his step on the stair. "We'll call you when we want you!" The quilts, hung on their safety-pin rings, made a gay and handsome curtain. "Looks pretty spiffy!" Mamma Young said; "now, don't it? I thought you'd like the red. I'll go down and send Ralph up." She went out, walking on her tiptoes and holding up her hands in mock surprise. Phyllis had not guessed she had so much fun in her.

Almost at once she heard Ralph's step on the stair again. She tossed the hammer into a box behind the quilt curtains and waited, her palms cupped round her elbows.

Ralph came in and stood a moment with his mouth open, looking around. He looked helplessly, almost reproachfully, at her.

"Ours," she said, and felt her eyes fill with tired tears. Dimly she saw him go to the bed and sit down with his hands hanging over his knees. She knew what he was thinking. He was remembering her dainty room in her father's house, the big room with the maple bed in the house he had built for her, the house he had lost, that Tom held so against

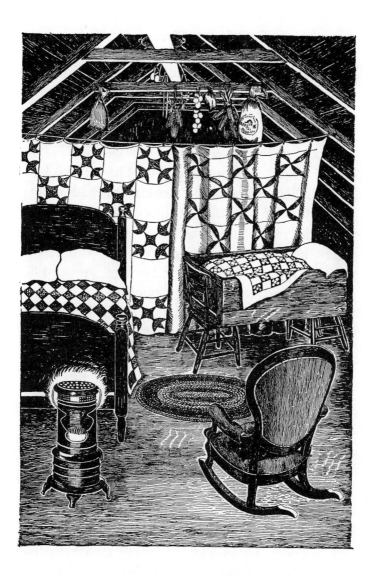

him. So many times she had seen him sit like that, after supper in the kitchen downstairs, sit and slowly shake his head. If she had fixed up the room when they first came he would have said something, would have protested against her working in the cold. Now he said nothing at all. She went to him and sat beside him, resting her clasped hands on his shoulder. She was tired too and leaned against him. "Wanta know something nice?" she said, in a voice they kept for foolishness. "Your brother Tom doesn't love his wife Edna, and he never, never did! Isn't that a sweetly solemn thought?"

"Ya, I guess that's right," Ralph said. "He wanted the little Drier girl. Like to never got over it."

Phyllis lifted one of his hands and laid it against her cheek. "How's m'old corn-picker?" she asked. "How's the wrist?"

"Oh, sore." He lay back on the bed and shut his eyes. "This is—nice," he said.

Phyllis rested her hand on his outflung arm. "And old Gran'ma'll never find us here," she said.

Ralph laughed in his throat and drew her to him. "I don't mind her," he said. "I like to hear her go on."

"Ralph!" Tom's voice came in exasperation up the well of the stairs. "Get on down here and eat.

34

We got to get out there."

Mamma Young put her head in from the dining-room. "Would you carry that boiler of water, off the stove, in here for me, Ralph? I'm going to give Gran'ma her bath."

Ralph carried in the boiler of water and emptied it into the tub beside the heater.

"It's too cold for me to take a bath," the old woman was protesting. "Mamie, I never bathed you, or any of you children, on such a cold day, You'll see."

"It's not cold in here, a bit," Mamma Young said patiently, "and I'll bathe you under a blanket."

"Oh, all right," old Grandma said. "I suppose I can't help myself, but you'll see."

In the kitchen Grandpa Young was slowly eating his dinner, his head resting against his left fist. Phyllis thought he looked very tired, and much, much older than Mamma Young.

"It's too cold to go out and pick, boys," the old man said, "and anyway, what there is you can pick in two days. Let it stand."

Ralph, when he had finished his dinner, sat still at the table, looking at the old man. Without thinking what he did he kept touching his sore wrist to his lips.

Phyllis filled her plate with food and then let it go almost untouched. She was very tired from her morning's work, and now that they were downstairs again, she felt some anger with Ralph—felt he might have said something in appreciation, might have felt something more than sadness and shame at his own inability to furnish a better place for her.

"I went in to see Walter," the old man said in the stillness. "He said last spring, he thought he could let me have something, but now he can't. I don't know how we're goin' to feed, the winter." The boys looked at him without saying anything. They were both surprised that their father should have thought Walter or anybody else would lend them money. "I helped Walter out back there, I helped him twice." He looked sadly out the window toward the cornfield, as though he looked down rows of years. "And he'd help me if he could." He chewed slowly awhile and said: "We'd better write Harvey." He took a large bite of pie and shook his head. The sight of the pie, eaten in such sadness, made Phyllis feel sick. She got up from the table and went upstairs. In her room in the ell she took off her shoes and got into bed, not between the sheets, but between the blankets, and lay shivering, her feet curled, like a child.

All the Youngs, in great need, waiting months and months to ask their baby, their darling, who had a good job, to help them out! Grandpa had chosen a moment when Mamma Young was out of the room to suggest to the boys that they write. There had been some little trouble when Harvey was home last; just what, the Youngs had kept to themselves, but they all felt touchy about asking anything of him. Phyllis had seen her younger brother-in-law only once—at her wedding. Ah, the wedding! She remembered how pretty her father's house had been with flowers. "Local belle, charming daughter of local banker, marries western ranchman at brilliant wedding," the foolish little home-town paper had said. How silly to call Ralph's wheat-farm a ranch! Now the farm was gone, the house they had built and all; and her father's bank— it wasn't really his, of course; he just ran it—was an empty building. She could see it as it had looked when she had stopped to see her father, the windows streaked with Hallowe'en soapings. A cousin had given her father a room in his house where he could sit and look down the street.

Would Harvey, with his good job and his bachelor apartment and his car, help them? A lot he cared, not to have written! He couldn't help but know

37

how things were in Nebraska. The bed was warmer and her stomach felt better. Crying, she fell asleep.

The squeaking of the door wakened her and she put out a warm hand and curled it in her husband's. "Why, how dark!" she said. "Is it late? I must have slept a long time."

"It's clouded over," Ralph said, and sighed deeply.

"What's the matter?"

"Oh—plenty!"

"What?"

He sat down on the bed beside her. "I had it out with Tom."

"About the boys?"

"No. We didn't get around to that. About the place."

"What place?"

"Both of them, his and mine. Edna started it. We were writing to Harve. I was writing, and Dad and Tom were telling me what to write, and Edna put in her say. Ah, I don't know what she said, but something like: 'Why don't you tell him why we have to ask, why we got in the hole?' and I said: 'Why did we?' and she started in, and Tom took it up then too, trying to smooth it out, and only made it worse. Said if he and Dad hadn't mortgaged Tom's place to start me out they'd have his place yet. Why, Dad himself was all for me buying that combine, you know he was. Lord, I guess I worked as hard on this place as he did. Threw it up to me about those two years in ag school. Lord, he coulda gone too if he'd had the gumption. Dad wanted him to go. That combine!"

Phyllis, looking into his face, remembered a night in their living-room on their own farm. He had been writing a letter to a school friend. She had caught him grinning and he quoted from the paper under his hand—Ralph was shyly proud of his wit: "And I've settled down now; I've got me wives and combines!"

"What did you say?" she asked.

"Oh, I blew up, I guess. I told him everything. Why, Phyllis, you know it was on his and Dad's say I bought that packing stock! Lot better'n any of us got sucked in. Did he think I wanted to come back here? Stick you off up here in a hole in the wall! He'd never atried the wheat-farm, himself. He had his chance. He was scared."

"Then what?"

"I hit him."

39

"Ralph!"

"Yeah. I socked him. Only thing I'm sorry for it wasn't out in the field."

"Ralph! What'd he do?"

"Nothing. He got up and came for me, and I hit him again. Then Mamma came in—" He laid his head down on her shoulder. There was something about the smell of his hair that made her think of her teaching days. More than one hot head had cooled against her shoulder after schoolyard scraps. "Well," he said, "he had it coming to him!"

"And Edna?"

"I don't know. I didn't think about her."

He turned and laid his cheek against hers. "You sore?"

"No, but it was bad for the folks. What about the letter?"

"Dad's finishing it up, I guess." Neither spoke for a while.

"Don't you think you ought to go for Betty if it's going to storm?"

Ralph did not answer. He had gone to sleep. She waited a little, slid her arm from under his head, got up, put on her shoes, and went downstairs.

Mamma Young was alone in the kitchen. "Edna's gone out to shut up the chickens," she said calmly.

40

"Arch thinks it's going to storm."

"Don't you think someone ought to go for Betty?" Phyllis asked.

"Arch's gone," was the answer. "Took the wagon." The old woman was standing at the kitchen window trying to thread a needle by the dim light. Phyllis took the needle from her hands and threaded it. "Thought I might as well mend gloves," Mamma Young said; "have 'em ready."

"Did Ralph hurt Tom—bad?"

"Oh—I don't think so. They were both pretty ashamed of theirselves, I think. Did he tell you— they were writing to Harvey? I was gettin' Gran'ma dressed after her bath and didn't know till I heard 'em scuffling. I hate for 'em to bother Harvey, but I guess it has to be."

Phyllis looked at her mother-in-law's face bent over the glove on her hand and wondered whether the boys would be relieved or disappointed to know that their coming to blows impressed their mother less than the letter to her baby.

"He's such a boy!" the old woman said. "He's got on well, but he's a free spender, too. I doubt if Harvey's got it to send. I wouldn't be surprised if he pretty well lives up what he makes. A boy not married, you know, he can't lay by much, there in

41

a city. Too many places for it. He'll be put out if he has to disappoint them."

"If he can't help, what'll they do?" asked Phyllis.

"God knows," Mamma Young said, and added: "—I trust."

There was the rattle of wheels on frozen ground, and Grandpa drove into the yard, got down over the wheel, stiffly, and put his arms up for Betty. Phyllis opened the door for her, and the child threw herself into her arms and began to sob loudly. Edna came in, her shoulders hunched under her shawl, and said sharply: "*Now* what's the matter?"

The second of her sons began to explain loudly and the other two chimed in. Phyllis listened, looking from one to another of them, her child's arms tightened about her neck. Betty was wearing her grandfather's cap. "They threw my cap up in a tree!" the child sobbed. "George did, and they wouldn't get it down."

"Aw, we couldn't!" George said, "the little old bawl-baby! We tried and tried to get it down. Tom was up in the tree when Gran'pa come along. We got let out early. George just tossed her old cap up there and she started in to bawl—"

Tom had come in. Phyllis noticed that his face was a little skinned, but not swollen. He heard only the end of his son's explanation. "You can get right back down that road and get that cap," he said hoarsely. "Get."

George began to whimper.

"Go on!" his father yelled; "get that cap, and no back talk."

The boy pulled on his cap and went to the door, crying. Edna stepped between him and the door. "Hang up your cap!" she said. "You're not going out in this." She looked defiantly at Tom.

"Get away from that door," Tom said.

"You make me!" Edna replied, her head drawn low between her shoulders.

Phyllis clasped her arms more tightly about Betty. Tom took a step toward Edna, and the child, frightened, screamed sharply. Tom swung about to look at Betty, and the door opened suddenly behind Edna, and Grandpa came in. "Going to storm, all right," he said; "glad the stock's all up."

Edna moved away from the door and said again to her boy: "Take off your things and hang 'em up!" The boy obeyed, looking sullenly from his mother to his father. Tom went to the table, sat down, and folded his arms. Phyllis let Betty down and stooped to take off her overshoes. Her sobbing had not stopped. It filled the kitchen.

43

Phyllis looked up at the clock and saw the white rectangle of the letter to Harvey behind it. It seemed startlingly white in the dusk of the room. The little boys were very quiet. Phyllis heard Tom's angry breathing between her child's sobs. "Never mind, never mind," she heard herself saying and realized she must have been saying it over and over.

"Come help me get in cobs," Grandpa Young said, and little Tommy went out with him.

Mamma Young was cleaning a lamp chimney with a piece of newspaper. She held it up to the dim light, blew in it, and wiped it with her apron. "There," she said when she set the lighted lamp on the table, as though she had fixed everything. "Now, girls, what'll we have for supper?" Neither of her daughters-in-law answered her. Edna went to the stove and put cobs on the fire, rattling the grate noisily.

Grandpa and little Tommy came in with cobs. "Let's milk early, boys," the old man said.

Tom got to his feet. "That somebody yellin'?" he asked his father.

"I thought I heard something," Phyllis said.

Tom turned and looked at her. She felt he was not angry with her, at least. "That's right," he said; "sure is," and went out on the step.

44

"Can't hear anything in here," Edna said, looking over her shoulder at the still crying Betty.

"It's somebody comin' in from the road," Mamma Young said, peering out. "Man and a woman, looks like."

"Car stalled, I expect," Grandpa said; "it's droppin' fast. Bet it'll be plenty cold tonight. Spitting snow now. Sharp as sleet."

The stair door opened and Ralph came into the kitchen, and almost on the same instant the outside kitchen door swung open and Mrs. Young came forward, smoothing her apron, to welcome whoever had come.

"Harve! Why, you old—" Ralph said loudly, and Mamma Young cried: "Harvey!" and threw her arms about the young man's neck. Grandpa came in, and while they were all greeting their youngest and dearest, Phyllis had time to take as good a look at the girl with him as the lamplight would allow. She was a small, very slender girl in a short gray fur jacket. Her slim, thin-stockinged legs were red and shivering with the cold. She moved toward the stove, took a violet handkerchief from her sleeve, and wiped her small nose. Yellow hair fell in disorderly crinkled strands over her cheeks.

It was Mamma Young who reminded her son of

45

the girl's presence. "Oh—this is Cleo," he said, and turned back to his brothers; "my wife," he added as an afterthought. Mamma Young put her arms about the girl and introduced her to Phyllis and Edna. Little Betty, through with crying, sat on the edge of her great-grandmother's bed in the corner and stared. The boys, all three, climbed into the woodbox, and stared too.

Helped out of his coat, Harve rubbed his hands above the range and said: "Sure didn't expect to see you here, Ralph. Driving back? Well, guess you'll have to wait till after the storm. Radio says it's going to blow a good one."

Before Ralph could answer, old Grandma tottered in from the dining-room, trailing a quilt about her shoulders. She came slowly round the table, one hand held out in front of her, her head thrust forward. "George!" she squeaked happily, "Georgie!" and let the quilt fall and held out her arms. "Hello, Gran'ma, how are you?" Harve said, and gave the old woman a hug.

"I dreamed it," she said; "I dreamed you was here." She patted his face.

"That's Harvey," Grandpa Young said in her ear, "that ain't George, Ma, that's *my* boy, Harvey." He put out his hand as though he would lay it on the head of a child of three or four years. "Harvey, *my* boy."

"Oh," the old woman said, loosening her arms from about Harvey. "And I thought you was George, my boy George. Went to Alaska, you know. So you're Arch's boy—you're Harvey? You are not! George, you're foolin'."

"Nope, I'm Harve, Gran'ma, sure am."

"Well, well." She stroked his hand. "I'd asworn, if I'd swear, you was George. You favor him. Who's this you brought home, Son? Who's this woman, George? You got a wife up there?" She came close to Harvey's wife and peered into her face. "I declare, girl," she cried, "what you done to your mouth?"

"That's make-up, Gran'ma!" Harvey yelled; "paint!" The girl's lip curled and she drew back. The old woman tucked down her chin and folded her hands on her stomach and said sternly: "George Young, have you brought home a strange woman?"

Harvey laughed. "Just a little strange, Gran'ma," he said, and at the horrified look his grandmother gave him he added: "She's all right."

Phyllis was helping Harvey's wife out of her coat. The lining was torn in the sleeve. When the girl took off her hat her half-length yellow hair fell about her shoulders. She twisted it up with tiny, red-nailed fingers.

Ralph led his grandmother to her bed and had her sit down. She seemed much shaken.

"Sure didn't expect to see you here, Ralph," Harvey said again. "Sure nice." Then: "Tom, you folks over for supper too? Regular family reunion."

Edna snorted.

"Yes, we're all here," Tom said loudly. "Better know it first as last. Had to let my place go. Ralph lost his. We're all here."

"That a fact?" Harvey said, looking from one to the other of them and then at his father.

"That's right, Son," the old man said guiltily; "it couldn't be helped. We've got just this place. Corn's better'n most around here, but it's not much. I don't know how we're going to feed the winter. I wrote you today."

"You're *flat*, Dad?"

"It looks like it, Son. Well, it's not quite that bad. I've still got my place here, and that's more than most around here."

The girl, who had been shivering by the stove and had said nothing at all, stepped suddenly into the circle of lamplight and cried shrilly: "Damn you, Harve Young, you do *this* to me!" She was

48

crying, with sudden sharp, angry sobs. "You drag me off out here!"

Mamma Young gasped.

"Oh, shut up, Cleo," Harvey said; he took her by the arms and tried to quiet her.

"Yes, we'd go to your folks, she screamed; "they've got a farm, a big house, plenty of room!"

Harve put his hand over his wife's mouth. "Shut up," he said evenly.

"Shut up yourself," she screamed against his hand, struggling, sobbing.

Tom placed a chair for her. "Sit down, won't you?" he said, and Phyllis was surprised at his concern, his politeness. The girl dropped into the chair and rested her sharp elbows on the table and cried the louder. Mamma Young started to go to her, to put an arm around her, and Harve said: "Don't touch her, Mamma; let her go." He backed toward the stove and stood near it, rubbing his cold hands up and down his legs. He looked around on the family. "I'm sorry," he said. "I've done everything I could. She's carried on the whole way."

"Did you have car trouble, Son?" his mother asked, trying to comfort him, trying to get away from the weeping girl and the tragedy, for all of them, her outburst revealed. "I haven't any car,

Mamma," Harvey said, like a child who wants to confess everything and be forgiven; "I haven't a thing. My job blew up four months ago. We—hitch-hiked."

"Yes," the girl screamed, " in all this cold, rode in trucks—everything! You lied, Harve Young—you said—"

"Shut up," Harve said again.

Tom stepped forward and put a hand on the back of the girl's chair. Phyllis saw his hand waver before it curved around the top of the chair-back, as though he would lay it on the girl's bright hair. "What's the matter with you?" he said to Harvey. "Is that any way to talk?"

Mamma Young touched Harvey's sleeve with her hand. "It's all right," she said, her voice trembling. "Ralph, will you get the boards out of the cellarway and help me widen the table? We'll get supper right away. Harvey, you'll feel better when you've had your supper."

Grandpa couldn't quite take it in. "You mean you've lost your job, Son?" he asked gently.

"Lost it!" Harve said; "the whole concern went under. Cleo worked in the office. I—we got married."

50

Ralph had brought the boards in. The girl had quieted a little. She half turned in her chair and rested an arm on the back of it, against Tom's hand, and sobbed. "He said to come here—he lied—he said—"

Harvey, still by the stove, groaned.

"Better get those galoshes off," Tom said; "looks like they're soaked." He came around in front of the girl, knelt awkwardly, and unfastened the small buckles. Edna, at the stove, was slicing potatoes into a sizzling skillet. In the dim light Phyllis saw her small eyes glint and her head lower between her thick shoulders.

Phyllis felt sick again. She moved toward the window, laid her cheek against the cold pane, and felt a little better. There was no more doubt about it now. In her mind she counted the winter months and then March and April. In May—not a good time for a farm baby, Edna would think.

Grandpa was saying something more about money, as though he were talking to himself. Old Grandma got up from her bed and came toward the table. "You're not to worry, Arch," she said soothingly. "It's all yours. I said to Pa, before he died: 'Don't split it up. Leave it every acre to Arch.

51

He'll take good care of it.'" She looked around on them. "George," she said, "did you bring a bucket of gold, or did I dream it?"

Tom set the small overshoes behind the range. "Better move up," he said to Cleo; "better move up to the fire and get warm."

Phyllis, at the window, shut her eyes. Now Ralph came to her, saw she didn't feel well, and put his arm about her. She let her weight rest against him. "Look," she said, nodding her head toward the lamp-flame reflected in the window. "When I was little, Father used to say, when I'd ask about it, 'twas a fire to warm all outdoors." His arm tightened. If he could only pick her up and carry her upstairs and put her in the bed, cover her up, and stay with her to comfort, away from all his people and the smell of food frying!

"Anyway, we're all here together," Mamma Young was saying, as though she were speaking to little children, "and supper'll be ready soon."

Old Grandma had come close to her son. "Arch, is that the wind I hear?" she asked; "is that the wind blowin' like that?"

Ralph turned and shouted to her over Phyllis's head: "It's the wind, Gran'ma, but *you* can't hear it!"

"I can feel it," the old woman said, "I can feel it to the bone, in this house. Is there fuel in, Arch? Weather like this don't clear overnight."

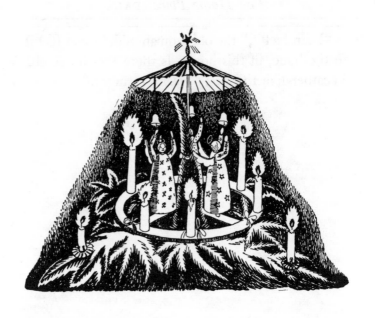

CHRISTMAS MORNING

FOR once Ralph woke before Phyllis, so that when she opened her eyes the room was already warmed and there was a yellow pattern of light on the rafters from the little oil heater they dressed by. Ralph was standing by the heater, dressed, rubbing his hands slowly up and down his legs to get the warmth through his cold clothes and into him. His lean face, with only the upward light on it, was older and sad and kind, like his father's.

54

Phyllis stirred, moved a little toward the edge of the bed, and he heard her at once and came to her. He bent over her and said: "Hello, Baby, how are you?"

"Fine," Phyllis said. "Merry Christmas, Love."

Ralph pressed his lips against the back of her limp hand. "You did too much last night, Baby. You should have let the other girls trim the tree. You mustn't *do* so much. You ought to let the other girls do things like that."

Phyllis slid a little closer to him. "You spoil me!" she said. "Anyway, Edna had enough to do. She was working on the dinner, doing all that could be done the night before, and Cleo wouldn't have a notion of how to trim a tree. I'm not sure Edna would either. And I *liked* it."

"Well, how *are* you?" Ralph asked again.

"You *know* how I am."

"How?"

"Happy," Phyllis whispered.

They had learned, in the month they had been sleeping in the attic room, to speak their waking thoughts in whispers, so as not to disturb their little daughter. Betty would be sleeping very lightly on Christmas morning.

"And how's the boy?" Ralph asked.

"All right. Only—I wish he was coming today. I wish he could be born on Christmas Day."

"Nope," Ralph said, his lips against her hand. "We have our babies in the spring, along with the rest of the farm. That's better."

"What kind of a day is it?"

"Pretty sharp," he replied; "pretty cold. I been up a good half-hour, and this place is barely getting warmed up now. Did you know I'd been up that long?"

"I didn't know," Phyllis said. "I was dreaming. I dreamed—why, it's gone! I've lost all but the very edge of my dream, and it was such a clear one, too."

"What's the edge?"

"Oh, I was home, I was little, about Betty's age, and at home. And Father was coming home from the bank and I ran to meet him. There was something especially happy about it. I've forgotten just what it was, though I'm sure it wasn't Christmas. It was a promise, I think."

Ralph laid his head against her and she knew, without his saying anything, that she had hurt him a little, that to himself he was remembering that she had had an adoring father who had brought her up in a handsome house and given her everything a little girl could wish. He was remembering that he,

56

her husband, had failed on his farm and brought her home, broke, to his people, to a little farmhouse much too small for the four families it housed.

"Poor Father!" Phyllis said. "They're good to him, but he'll be lonely. I wrote him a long letter. I thought I'd not tell him until later—until nearly time for the baby to come. But I did. I wanted to give him something, if only a secret. Besides, I'm happy and he'll see that in my letter." She wanted to remind Ralph that her father had failed too, along with the rest, and had nothing to do but stand at his window and fiddle with his watch-chain or walk down Main Street past an empty bank-building.

"Betty's waking!" Ralph said, and went to the child where she lay in her box-on-two-chairs bed. "Hi, Pet," he said.

The child put up wavering, sleepy arms. "Hi, Daddy," she said. "Is it Christmas?"

"You're darn tootin' it's Christmas!" His arms went tight about the tiny body.

"Mother," she cried, "it's Christmas!" She struggled to get free from her father's arms. "Let me down! Let me go, Daddy! It's Christmas!"

"Here!" Ralph said, and gave her a gentle spank to quiet her. "You want to wake up those three hyenas? You want to wake Edna's boys up? Come on; Daddy'll go down with you. Be a good joke on 'em. You'll see the tree first."

"Are you sure the fire's going good?" Phyllis asked. "Are you sure it's warm down there, Ralph?"

"Sure, Dad's been up an hour. Edna and Mamma are up too. I bet old Gran'ma's up. She wakes before anybody. She don't want to miss anything." He chuckled, thinking of his old grandmother and her ways, and Phyllis felt that vexation she always felt at his fondness for the old woman.

Little Betty was dancing about. Suddenly she streaked past her father, her nightgown fluttering, and Ralph was after her, crying, "Hey, Pet, where you *going*?" Phyllis heard squeals of laughter and fatherly kisses and knew that he had caught her at the top of the stairs and that their wish to see the tree before Edna's boys woke was defeated by their own foolishness. She nestled deeper into the warmth of the feather bed. Ralph and his mother and father would see to things for Betty, make her Christmas morning right. She knew she ought to get up, ought to go down and help, but she had tired herself the night before, trimming the tree. She had worked all day making candy too. And it had been hard working in the kitchen with Edna. All her efforts— and she was a good enough cook, a better cook than

58

Edna, actually—were made to look foolish and childish. Edna was getting ready for the Christmas dinner, and she made Phyllis feel in the way. Mamma Young could work with Edna without friction. In the work of the house there was a kind

of understanding between Edna and Mamma Young, an agreeable, sensible understanding that put the meals first.

Phyllis, thinking of Edna and her life of hard work and no thanks, wondered how *she* would live her life at all if Ralph felt toward her as Tom felt toward Edna. And how would she endure it if Ralph treated her as Harvey treated Cleo? She remembered a night in their own home, on their own farm, where everything had been right for her and Ralph. They were at table, she and Ralph and the hired girl and the two hired men, and she had said something that evidently, to the men, had a quite different meaning from her intention. One of the men had snorted his laughter, then choked. She had looked to Ralph and found him shaking with laughter too, silent laughter. She jumped up from the table and ran into her room. Ralph followed her and said, his arms about her: "But what you said was so *funny*, Baby! See? It was nothing, nothing at all. It just struck us funny, the way you said it. Just dumb men, that's all. You forget it." "But Olga!" Phyllis wept; "*she* laughed too." "Well, *she* understood. You're *different*, Phyllis. You've been raised in a glass house. I used to think, before I married you, I'd *larn* you something, but I gave it up. You see what happens when the hind marries the pure little, spoiled little princess, and no help for it." "I'm no such thing! That's simply nonsense!" Phyllis had wept, already wrapped round again in the love that made it possible for her to breathe. "I'm your *wife*!" "Right you are, and a darn good one," Ralph had

60

said. "And now you won't cry any more, will you, Baby? I've got to get out to my chores." She *had* cried more, a little, when he had gone. But she had stopped to wonder about the thing that had happened to her. She had not been able to tell him, she would have been ashamed had she had the words, that her world had slid quite out from under her because her husband had seemed to let go of his love for her for just an instant, for just long enough to laugh at her with Olga and the two hired men.

She was a spoiled girl, who lived on love, but she was a good wife, too. What would she do if Ralph treated her as Tom treated Edna, as Harvey treated Cleo? "I'd die," she said aloud, and stretched a little, nestled deeper into the bed, and fell asleep.

When she woke, someone was rapping sharply at her door. She was astonished to see her young new sister-in-law, Cleo, standing there with her blue brocaded pyjama jacket wrapped tightly around her shivering self. "Phyllis," Cleo said in her high plaintive voice, "can I come in? Can I get in with you?"

Phyllis lifted the covers for Cleo to get in beside her. She hugged the cold, shivering girl close to her.

"How'd you happen to get up so early?" Phyllis asked. "Is Harvey up? Are they *all* up now?"

"Ralph got us up," Cleo said. "We were asleep, we were *trying* to sleep, and those brats of Edna's were howling around out there, around the tree, and Ralph came in *carrying* old Grandma Young."

"Into *yours and Harvey's* room?"

"Yes! He said: 'Here, you! Gran'ma wants in her own bed on Christmas morning. You kids get up now and let Gran'ma have her bed.' Then *you* know, you know what she'd say: She said, she said to Harvey—Ralph holding her there like a baby; she looked down at us and said to Harvey: 'George, who's *that*? Who *is* that woman?' About *me*, see?" Though her back was to Phyllis and her yellow hair all that Phyllis could see of her head, she knew how Cleo had tightened her lips like an old woman's in saying Grandma's speech. "Gosh, this sure is a Christmas!" she finished.

Both girls laughed a little, Cleo very bitterly. With her arm about Cleo's slender shoulders Phyllis lay thinking of her husband's people. For the moment, because she had come to her to get warm, to talk a little about the Young family's babying of old Grandma, Phyllis felt some love for Cleo. That Cleo was hard and ugly-natured and would not help at all with the work she forgot for a little. She felt sympathy for her. The Youngs did seem so all-to-themselves in their humoring of old Grandma, in their delight at her everlasting insistence that her youngest grandson Harvey was her own son George. Ralph never failed to "get a kick" out of her notion that Cleo was a heathen woman George had picked from a mission in the Klondike.

"Did you stop by the tree?" Phyllis asked. "Did you open your presents?"

"No," Cleo answered. "I know what mine is already. Socks! *Bed*-socks. Mamma Young knitted them, out of yarn from an old shawl, or something."

"They'll be nice," Phyllis said, and drew her arm from around Cleo.

"Oh, sure," Cleo agreed. "I didn't mean *that*. I meant—I think Harvey didn't get me anything." Her voice rose, pained, angry.

"How could he?" Phyllis defended her youngest brother-in-law. "There's no money. The cream money was just for the stamps to send letters and for the stuff for the candy. Did you get *him* something?"

"Yes."

"What?"

"You wait; you wait and see!" Cleo was always telling people to wait and see, as though she felt sure of reckonings when she would come out on top.

"Where's Edna?" Phyllis asked.

"Kitchen, I guess, getting breakfast."

"And Tom?"

"Outside, I guess." Cleo half turned toward Phyllis and brushed the hair back from her forehead with her thin fingers. "Oh," she said, her voice suddenly gentle, "you know what Tom did? He got skates for his boys, all three! *Ice* skates."

"Skates! Why, *how?*"

"I don't know. They were trying them on when I went through to the kitchen. They're going down to the river to skate."

"But how?" Phyllis asked. "There wasn't any money left."

"*I* don't know," Cleo said, almost whining. "You wait. You'll see . . ." her voice trailed off. She was almost asleep.

Phyllis did not like the morning smell of face powder and tobacco about Cleo's neck and hair. She got up, sliding carefully round Cleo, and went to stand by the stove while she dressed. She put on her red wool dress that little Betty liked so much. In the mirror over the dresser she saw that she looked rested and pretty enough. Her dark hair curled softly around her ears, and her eyes were bright. She quietly made Betty's little bed, turned the oil stove out, opened the small window, and went downstairs.

Betty slid from her place on her grandfather's knee by the kitchen stove and ran to her, her arms full of gifts. "Look!" she screamed. "Look at my

Christmas! And come look here!" Her arms were too full for her to take her mother's hand, but she danced ahead into the dining-room.

"Look at my table and chairs!" she cried, almost beside herself with joy. "Gran'pa made them! He sawed them and hammered them and put them together and painted them and everything!"

Grandpa Young followed, sheepishly, to see

65

Phyllis's pleasure in his gift to his little granddaughter. "Yes, sir," he said, after whistling a little through his teeth. "Yes, sir, I always thought a little girl should have a red table and chairs. My sister, my sister Dora, she had a little red table and two chairs Pa made for her. Good work, too; fancier than these here. I didn't have the right paint for them. Had to use what we had on hand. I like a brighter red, for a little girl's table and chairs. This just some was on the place."

Betty dropped everything and ran to climb her grandfather and kiss his face and neck. While he held her tightly, she threw her head back so that her throat was an arch, and cried: "Gran'pa, I love you more than all the trees and all the houses in all the world!"

Phyllis slid her fingertips over the shining tabletop. She saw as in two mirrors a recession of little Young girls, for generations and generations, standing by little red tables their grandfathers had made for them. She saw her daughter's daughter, too, standing by her little red table.

Her mother-in-law had come into the room, still breathing hard from making up her feather bed. "What time is it, Phyllis?" she asked. "Don't you feel good?"

"I feel fine," Phyllis said. "I feel a little light-headed, but I feel fine. I feel I came into the king-dom to have little Young girls standing by little red tables, world without end, amen!"

Her mother-in-law put a warm, strong-under-soft arm about her and said: "I know how you feel. You need your coffee. You overdid yesterday. Have you looked at your presents? Well, come have your breakfast first. You look kind of wobbly to me."

"I feel fine," Phyllis said again, and allowed her-self to be led into the kitchen.

The menfolk had come in from the stables and were just sitting down to breakfast. "Merry Christ-mas!" her brothers-in-law greeted her, and Harvey, who was less shy than Tom, got up from his place and came round to her and kissed her soundly on the mouth. She put up her hand and patted his firm lean cheek. The Young men looked on approvingly, wishing in their hearts, Phyllis knew, that Harvey, the youngest and tallest, had such a wife as Ralph's.

"How do you want your egg?" Edna spoke from over the stove. Phyllis, in the warmth of greetings from the menfolk, had forgotten Tom's wife.

"It's Christmas. We get our eggs to order this morning," Ralph explained.

"That's nice," Phyllis said. "But I'm late, Edna.

67

Let me fix my own breakfast."

"Just as you like," Edna said, tiredly, and brought her own well-loaded plate and sat down by her husband. Tom frowned. Phyllis could see he was vexed and ashamed that Edna had not gone ahead and fixed Phyllis's egg after she had said she would. Edna ate and did not lift her eyes.

"I'll fix your egg, Phyllis," Ralph said, "and I know how you want it." He reached for his sister-in-law's apron-string, gave it a yank, and pulled the apron from around Edna's heavy hips. "Merry Christmas, Edna!" he said loudly. "Gosh all Friday, it's Christmas!"

Edna gave her snorting laugh, and her mouth quivered at the corners a little when the laugh was gone. She suffered at the unfamiliar red that came to her face.

"Oh, why doesn't he *love* her?" Phyllis thought in anger. "Why doesn't Tom *love* Edna? How can she bear it, how can she stand Christmas or any other day, without him loving her? How can he half love Cleo instead—little, skinny, and mean as she is—when Edna is here, strong and kind and willing under her harshness? Why doesn't he go to her and be sweet to her and see what happens? Maybe she'd bloom, like a—like a *cabbage!*" She began to laugh to herself.

"What's the joke, Baby?" Ralph asked. "Here's your coffee, and your poached egg'll be along in a minute."

"We're going skating," Tom said. "The little boys are down to the river already. Hope they don't break their necks."

"Yeh," Harvey said. "Where do you suppose Dad found those old skates? 'Member the Christmas we got them, Tom? You and Ralph taught me between you—and you let me drop now and then, doggone you, for the fun of it. It was a morning like this, about; wasn't it? Cold, snow underfoot, a little, but the ice was clean."

Tom smiled. "A-uh," he said. "We sure made Mamma mad. We took Harve, he couldn't abeen but around six, down to the river and we skated up and down all day, about. Brought him home with such a leg-ache he bawled all night. Had croup, too, didn't you, Harve?"

"Don't remember a thing about it but the skating," Harvey said.

"And here's your egg, Duchess!" Ralph said, carrying the plate high on spread fingers.

"Papa found them in the cellar, or in the old tool-chest, or somewhere," Tom went on; "sharpened 'em up and fitted 'em to the kids' shoes last night. When they got up, there was the skates on their shoes."

Edna smiled a little. Grandpa had done something for *her* boys, something that was almost as much work as making a little table and two chairs for Betty, his favorite.

"How'd you like to come down to the river with us?" Ralph asked his wife. "We'll build a good fire. I'd take along a blanket for you to wrap around you. You'd not get cold. You could sit and watch."

"Why, I can *skate*," Phyllis said. "I'm a good skater. And my skates are in my trunk. I brought them along."

"Swell! Harvey said. "We'll all skate."

"I can skate too," Edna said, but no one heard her in the general pleasure over Phyllis's being able to skate, over her having thought to bring her skates along.

Old Grandma Young had come into the kitchen and was making her trembling way toward the breakfast table.

"Hello, Gran'ma!" Ralph yelled at her deafness. "Merry Christmas! Want another breakfast?"

The old woman put out her hands to him, to be led. "Another?" she said, and drew a long face.

70

"Why, you smarty, I've not had my first yet. *Is* it Christmas Day? I guess it is. It must be something like that. I woke up in my own bed. Yes, I did. I been shoved around from pillar to post in this house. Pa left me to my boy Arch. He said, his last words: 'Arch, you look after your mother!' and I thought he would. He has, I guess, best he can. But here in my old age where do I sleep? I got a good bed of my own, but can I sleep in it? No. No, I might be an old shoe. I can sleep in the kitchen corner, me and the cat. Some *woman* sleeps in my bed, some young woman. She sleeps in there with one of you boys, and I'm going to speak to your father about it!"

Ralph laughed and patted his old grandmother's knee. "Aw, Gran'ma," he yelled, "you're foxy, but you can't fool me. You'd like us to think you're fuddled, but you're not. You're clear as a bell. You know just what you're saying. You're *all right!*"

"Why, I am not!" the old woman said, laughed a little, and looked round on them all. "*Acourse* I'm all right, though it's enough to mix up anybody to get moved from their own bed, like I been. But I *was* in my own bed *this* morning. I woke up in it. I was dreaming. I was dreaming about my boy George." She turned to Phyllis and touched her wrist with the handle of her spoon. "You know, I lost my boy," she confided; "my youngest son. I had a fine boy, grown up, just grown to manhood, twenty-two he was, taller'n any in this house, and he said: 'Ma, I'm going to Alaska, where the gold is,' and you know, nothing could hold him, not his pa, or not me. He was set on going. I said to his pa: '*Talk* to him, Pa; see if you can't swing him to stay home'; but no, nothing could swing him to stay. He said, when I wouldn't let up beggin' him to stay: 'We'll say no more about it, Ma,' and then—he went. If his *father* said: 'We'll say no more about it,' I always knew where I stood about anything, but not with my boys. He went away up there and—say, where's that *woman?* Did he send her back?"

"What woman, Gran'ma?" Ralph baited.

The old woman creased the edges of the oilcloth table-cover. "I can't say," she said, deeply confused. "There was a woman George brought home here. It was a mistake, I guess."

Harvey sighed deeply. "Where *is* Cleo?" he asked.

"Oh, she's up in my room, sleeping," Phyllis said. "Do you think she'd like to go skating with us?"

"No, let her sleep," Harvey said.

Mamma Young came into the kitchen with her hand on little Betty's shoulder. "Well, I hope I've got this girl away from that tree long enough to eat her breakfast," she said. "I got her dressed and dished up breakfast for her when Edna's boys had theirs, but she was so excited I think she hardly ate a bite— Why, Gran'ma *Young*, what're you *doing*, eating another breakfast?"

"Why, Mamie, what's wrong with you? This is my first breakfast. I woke in my bed, my own bed, and—"

"No, you didn't, Gran'ma," Mamma Young said kindly enough; "you *woke* in the kitchen, and I washed you and got you dressed and gave you your breakfast, and then Ralph came down and carried you in and put you into your own bed in your room."

"Well, it's time!" old Grandma said, and began to cry a little. "I shouldn't ever abeen yanked outa it."

"Now, Ma," Grandpa Young said, "you don't need to talk that way. You try and think back and you'll remember it was *your* idea. When things went bad and the young folks came home, they had to have a room, and you said: 'Here, they can have *mine*. I'd just as soon sleep in the kitchen.'"

"Well, what if I *did*!" Old Grandma wept. "What of it? You've no business to hold me to it,

73

just because I made that offer. I'm an old woman. I've lived a hard life and I've never held back or shirked. Last words your pa said was: 'Arch, you look after your mother,' and now here I have to sleep in the kitchen! I may go any day, any night, and am I to be taken, sleepin' in the *kitchen*?"

Mamma Young patted old Grandma on the shoulder. "You come in and see the tree, Gran'ma," she said, "and you tell little Betty, here, about Christmas when you were a girl in Indiana."

The old lady brought her hands down flat on the table. "We *made* Christmas!" she cried, "and you don't know the meaning of it. There was something *to* it. We begun around Thanksgiving, for I had a German grandmother, as well as my Irish one, and not a cookie would we children get to see. Everything was hid away. You'd look at a door, a closet door, and you'd no more opened it than anything. Everything was secret. You'd think you'd be struck dead if you put your hand on the knob."

"And didn't you ever peek, Gran'ma, not *once*?" Ralph asked.

The old woman nodded. "Acourse I did!" she said. "Silas and I peeked. He was my cousin, and he wore his hair still in long curls. We peeked into the kitchen and saw cookies spread all over the table, stars and pipes, and flowers and birds, with seed and red sugar on them. The cookie-cutters were there too, the old German ones."

"And did you get struck by lightning?"

"Not then! It was winter, and if you don't think they have winter in Indiana, you're wrong. They do. It can get bitter cold. And the Christmas tree! We had all those trimmings from Germany that were my grandma's, my ma's ma. Silver angels at the top, over candlesticks, and when the candles were lighted, the angels begun to move round and round, from the heat of the candle flames, and going round they touched three little bells and made chime-music, sweet as anything."

Betty slid from her chair and came to her great-grandmother's side. "And did they *sing?*" she breathed. "Did they sing: 'Glory to God in the highest'?"

"Where *are* those things—the cookie-cutters and the tree-trimmings?" Grandpa Young asked. "Who'd they go to, Ma?"

"Why, I don't know, Son. But they didn't come to me and your pa. I guess they went to some of Aunt Kate's folks. Law me! I guess, of souls living, I'm the only one to recall and tell of it. A boy like Silas, with such curls, such a hardy boy! They

75

killed him in the war, I guess. Yes, that's what happened to him. In '63 that was, he was killed. But we stood there in the kitchen door, so bold, and holding hands, the door wide open, and looked, but we neither of us touched a cookie. It didn't come into our minds."

"Well, if we're going skating, hadn't we better get going?" Tom asked. "Get your skates, Phyllis; they'll probably need a little honing."

"Why, what are you *saying!*" old Grandma cried. "Mamie, isn't this the girl who's going to have a child? Well, she's *not* to go skating. 'Twould be a piece of foolhardiness. You stay home, my dear."

"Will you get up and give me a chance at the table?" Edna asked loudly. "I got a big dinner to get, and I can't do a thing with you all in the kitchen."

"Yes, Edna's right," Mamma Young said. "I don't know when I've known you to linger at the table so. I guess you're having a good time. Arch, isn't it good to have them all here together? And all so well and strong. We've got *that*. There's no sickness in the house this year."

"Yes," old Grandma said, "it's 'cause we've had such a good cold winter and the frost cleared the air of sickness. A good freeze and that blizzard.

Didn't we have a blizzard, Son?"

"Why, we had blizzard *on* blizzard, Gran'ma!" Ralph said.

"Shoo! Get out, all of you," Mamma Young said, "and don't come back till two. We'll have dinner around two o'clock. Phyllis'll stay here and help. Gran'ma's right. She shouldn't be skating. Might be all right and it might not."

"Do you want to go along, Pet, or do you want to stay by the tree?" Ralph asked Betty.

His daughter stood twisting her clasped hands. The decision was hard for her. "The tree!" she cried at last. "I'll *stay by the tree!*"

When he had put on his sheepskin and cap, Ralph kissed his wife and child and followed his brothers out into the cold of the morning. Phyllis stood by the window and watched them go, the three of them running, their skates over their shoulders.

"Fine men, those Young boys!" she said to her mother-in-law, and they laughed proudly together.

"Come into the dining-room before we start clearing up the dishes," Mamma Young said, "and you come too, Edna. Phyllis hasn't seen her presents yet."

"Thanks. I got things to do," Edna said.

Little Betty skipped ahead to open the door, and

to dance around the tree and take down her mother's presents for her.

"Why, how'd I get so *many*?" Phyllis asked when they were piled in her lap.

"Because you're prettiest!" Betty said, and was suddenly embarrassed and buried her face in her grandmother's apron and twisted her little backside and giggled.

"The bed-socks I made all the same stitch, for each you girls," Mamma Young said. "I wanted so to get new yarn and have 'em each a different color, but that was out of the question, acourse, so I got out that old shawl that Jenny, my best friend when I was a young woman, Jenny, knit for me. The place the moths had been in it was just in one corner, and the rest was still perfectly good. I'd have picked red for you if I could have picked. It's a warmer color."

"Why, a mirror!" Phyllis cried when she unwrapped Ralph's present.

"Yes, a hand mirror," Mamma Young said. "Ralph was going to make it himself, when he found that nice hardwood board from an old bedstead that was mine when I first married, and that square of looking-glass, but Arch thought he'd like to do it, and Ralph knows his father is far and away a

78

better hand with tools than he is. Isn't the carving nice? Ralph found a picture of the way he'd like it, and Arch did the carving for him. Isn't that as natural a rose as you ever saw?"

"It's lovely," Phyllis said, and threw back her head, looking in the mirror and smoothing her hair with her palm. Her cheeks were redder than usual and her eyes bright.

"Now mine, mine, mine!" Betty demanded.

The paper on Betty's present to her mother was badly wrinkled and the ribbon twisted. It was plain the package had been tied and untied many times.

"A tray!" Phyllis said. She had seen the tray more than once and had promised over and over to forget it absolutely and be surprised on Christmas morning. "Why, it's the prettiest tray I've ever seen!"

"For pins!" Betty cried, and reached up and took a pin from her grandmother's bosom and dropped it into the tray with a flourish. "We made them in school."

"Thank you, darling," Phyllis said; "it's lovely."

"Lovely, lovely, lovely," Betty sang, and began to hop around the tree on one foot.

"We'd better get out to the kitchen," Mamma

79

Young said; "we mustn't let Edna do it all alone."

"Oh, the dinner, the dinner!" Betty sang. "We *still* have the dinner!"

"And in the evening the apples and nuts and candy," Mamma Young said, "don't forget that. Your mother made the candy. You must write all the receipts out for me, Phyllis. That's something I never learned, to make candy. Plain taffy's all my boys ever got, but they used to like that. You must write them all out."

"Yes," Phyllis said, "before I go away. Do you suppose we'll ever go away? Think you'll have your house cluttered with us forever, Mamma Young? You've made us all such a welcome. We forget, really, how much you do, how much you put yourself out for us."

The red washed over Mamma Young's face, and her eyes brimmed. "Why, Phyllis, you fuss me so!" she said. "Don't talk that way! I don't put myself out. They're my boys, and you girls are their wives. And I'm mighty thankful I've been spared, till now. Last winter, you know, I had the quinsy, and I did think, myself, I was going, and I hung on so. I couldn't help but feel I'd be needed yet, by more than Arch and Gran'ma. If things stay bad, like they are, I may be needed even worse. I want to be here when your baby comes. And—you're a *daughter* to me, Phyllis."

They looked into each other's eyes, and Phyllis saw all the hurt Mamma Young had known, and would never know less because two of her sons had married badly.

"You're right for Ralph," Mamma Young said, the tears running over. "That's something to stay us, Arch and me, that you and Ralph are together, and have Betty and this one that's coming."

Betty had been playing on the other side of the tree. Now she came to her mother and asked: "Who's coming? Is somebody coming for Christmas?"

"I'll go out and help Edna," Mamma Young said; "there's a lot to do."

"I'll come in a minute," Phyllis said, and sat down on one of the little red chairs at Betty's Christmas table.

"Ah, I'll pour you some tea, Mrs. Lady," Betty said stylishly, and spread her skirts round her, lifted her shoulders, and pursed her mouth. "It's a lovely day, isn't it?"

"Indeed it is, Mrs. M'Honey," Phyllis said in a lady voice, "but I think it's going to snow, don't you?"

"I declare, it *is* snowing," Betty said, "and it's as fine as sugar."

> "Snowflakes may be like sugar
> Or like sand.
> Snowflakes may be like pieces of wool,
> Like feathers,
> Like breath,
> Or like stars in the hand,"

Phyllis quoted.

Betty looked at her mother over the edge of her little cup and said in her everyday voice: "Mother, do you suppose Mamma Young would mind if I named my doll Jesus?"

"I don't know, dear," Phyllis said. "She *made* the doll for you, so perhaps you'd better ask her. I think she wouldn't care. In Mexico they name their real babies Jesus."

"*Do* they? Just their Christmas babies, or babies any time?"

"Their anytime babies."

"And are they *good* people?"

"Yes, of course."

"I thought Mexicans were some of the bad people."

"Oh, no, they're good. All people are good."

82

"Why, *Mamma*! They aren't really. There *are* bad people!"

"Yes, of course, but they aren't any special kind."

"They're all mixed up, aren't they?"

"Yes."

"Cleo gave me the dishes, Mother. She gave me this whole tea-set."

"She did! That's nice."

"But, *Mother*—" Betty leaned across the table, narrowed her eyes, put her hand on her mother's wrist, and said: "*Where did she get the money?*"

"Oh, darling, don't say that, don't talk like that! It's Christmas, and everyone's been grand to you. Grandpa made you the table and chairs, and Mamma Young made you a doll, and I made you your new dress. You must just be happy on Christmas and not think about money."

"I *know*," Betty said, "but where *did* she get it, Mamma? Do you think they cost a dollar?"

"I don't know, Love," Phyllis said. "I expect someone sent it to her in a letter. You must thank her, first thing, when she gets up."

"Let's go out and help with the dinner," Betty said like a grown person. She got up and stretched herself and smoothed the hair back from her face in a gesture like her mother's.

The kitchen was full of good smells. There was a mingling of mince and sage, of burning cobs, of new bread.

"Now come look, Betty," Mamma Young said; "come look at the goose all stuffed and ready. See, she's all sewed up! Open the oven door for Gran'ma. Careful, careful, Sweet. Don't burn yourself."

"You can go down and fetch up the jelly and jam and pickles, if you want," Edna said to Phyllis.

"I'll go too and help fetch," Betty said, and ran to the cellar door.

"Take a pan, take a bake-pan, to carry the stuff in," Mamma Young said.

On the dark stairs, her hand in her mother's, Betty whispered over and over: "Fetch, fetch, fetch!"

"What are you saying, dear?" Phyllis asked.

"I think I'm saying 'fetch,' " Betty said, "but I'm not sure. If you say a word a lot of times it gets bigger and bigger or it gets littler and littler and then it goes *out*. Doesn't it for you, Mother? You don't know if it's the word you started with, pretty soon. It sounds awfully funny. Is 'fetch' really *fetch*, Mother?"

"Yes," Phyllis said; "we're going to fetch the

jams and pickles and jelly. And let's find some piccalilli. There's a word for you."

Betty, at the foot of the cellar stairs, threw herself backward on some sacks of potatoes and lay
there, her arms spread wide, her eyes shut, saying
"piccalilli," over and over.

"Get up," Phyllis said. "It's cold down here. Let's
get the stuff, Betty."

Betty got up and stretched to see the labels on the
jam jars. "Well, it's kind of *warm* cold, don't you
think, Mother? It smells warm down here, don't
you think?"

"I think you're going to have a nap after dinner,"
Phyllis said.

Betty turned and looked up at her mother with
the quickly adjusted hurt look little girls give grown-
ups when they find themselves alone in their childhood again after, for a moment, having shared it.
"Yes, let's fetch the jams and stuff," she said
brightly.

When they had filled the pan they went upstairs.
Mamma Young opened the door for them. "Well!
Would you look at *that*!" she said, raising her hands
high for Betty's pleasure. "Did you pick and choose
all those, Sweet?"

Betty had had enough of grown folks' ways. She

nodded gravely and went into the dining-room, to her table and dishes and her doll.

"My, girls, we oughtn't to complain of anything," Mamma Young said, "with a cellar full like this. It makes me a little ashamed, yes, it really does, though goodness knows Edna and I worked hard enough putting the stuff up. I wish we could share it. Last year and other years I sent good big boxes of jam and fruit and stuff to all Arch's nephews and to others, but this year we just hadn't the sending money for it. They'll understand. The boxes to the church was all we did this year. Would you like to peel potatoes now, Phyllis?"

"I'll peel them, and Phyllis can set the table," Edna said. "We'll eat in the dining-room today, won't we, and use the big cloth?"

"Yes, yes, of course," Mamma Young said, "and you can fetch the table-cloth and napkins from the chest in my room, Phyllis. Edna did them up so nice. You're a wonderful ironer, Edna."

Edna sniffed her pleasure in the praise. "My mother was a good ironer," she said. Then: "We're going over there for New Year's Day. We're going over to my brothers'."

"Your brothers'?" Phyllis asked.

"Why, yes, I got folks," Edna said shortly. "I

got five brothers, three of them still to home, batching. I want to go over and bake them up some stuff. All right if I take some can-stuff?"

"Of course, of course," Mamma Young said, "and take some chickens, too, Edna. Bake them up some chickens before you go, why don't you? You'll take your boys along?"

"I guess so. My brothers like to have them. They like to tussle with 'em and take 'em hunting. There's no school till Monday after. They'd as well go along."

Phyllis went into Mamma Young's room to get the big table-cloth and the napkins. They were beautifully ironed and wrapped in blue tissue paper. How nice to think of Edna and her boys being away for even one day, for New Year's Day! For a day or two she would not have to see Edna's lumpy shoulders and hear her voice—and the boys would be away—little Betty would be free from their rough teasing. Maybe she would stay several days, if she meant to do a lot of baking for her bachelor brothers. Maybe there, among her own people, was the place Edna bloomed. Maybe there she was really at home.

Mamma and Grandpa Young's room was a little like Phyllis's own with its bright quilts and braided rugs. The bed looked especially good. Phyllis wanted to get into it and go to sleep. She was tired, and the day barely under way.

When she came out to the dining-room with the table-cloth, she found that Mamma and Grandpa Young had already widened the table, had put in the leaves. Old Grandma was excited by having her say about the day and about the meal. The cloth, careful as they were in laying it, was not quite "right with the world" and had to be lifted and laid again. Betty squealed with delight to see it billow when it was lifted.

"I'll bring holly from my trunk," Phyllis said, and went into old Grandma's room, that had been hers and Ralph's and little Betty's when they first came to the Young home place, to get the paper holly from a box in the trunk-till.

Mamma Young came in while she was still hunting for it. "Well, never mind it, Phyllis," she said. "Never mind if you can't find it. The food is pretty, alone, and the goose and cranberries and pickles and all make it kind of decorated. Anyway, the men and boys will be so hungry, with all this skating, they'll not notice much. They'll just want to *eat*." Mamma Young laughed and looked away to the snowy windows.

88

"Why are you laughing?" Phyllis asked.

"Oh, I guess I'd be ashamed to say. Your looking for the holly for the table and me telling you not to mind brought something to my mind, that's all. It made me think of when I was first married."

"What?"

"Oh, just *that*. The hours and hours and yards of work I did to have my clothes pretty."

"And wasn't Gran'pa pleased with them?"

Mamma Young creased her apron in neat tucks. "Oh, I guess so," she said, "when he got around to it. Come on. I ought to be in the kitchen. The men'll be hungry."

"Hungry or no hungry," Phyllis said, "here's the holly, and they'll get that too, along with their meal, and they'd better like it."

"My, it sure looks nice," Grandpa Young said to his wife. "You set an awful good table, Mamie, you always have, in lean times and plenty. I don't know how you've managed, but you have."

"Well, I guess you weren't starved when you were a *boy*! "Old Grandma Young bristled.

"I went down toward the river, walked part way down, this morning," Grandpa said, "and you know, Mamie, it was a funny thing. Those three boys of Tom's put me in mind of our three the Christmas

I got their skates for 'em. And yet there's *our* three too, grown and all well and hearty, skatin' along with 'em. Though, acourse, Tom's boys are closer together, in size, than our three were."

"Did you know, Phyllis," Mamma Young said, "I guess I never told you, but we lost two little boys, between Tom and Ralph. I'll show you baby Archie's picture some time. The other we didn't have taken, and how I wish we had! Oh dear!"

"Well, that's the way it is," old Grandma said. "I remember the boys you lost, Mamie. Just this last instant I recall one of them clear. Little fellow lyin' on my lap. I remember holding him just after you'd bathed him and you'd gone to fetch his gown, and so slippery on my knee. I could hardly hold him. I remember I said to you: 'Mamie, you'll never raise this child. He's too fair.' Well, that's the way it is. You lost two. I had nine, isn't that right, Son? I had nine, and I've lived to see them all laid away but Arch here. One I didn't see laid away—my youngest, George. And I can't lay him away in my mind, either. The door opens and I catch my breath. I think I'll look up and see him there. He went away to the Klondike. Aren't all my children gone but you, Arch—you and Mamie?"

"Yes, Ma," Grandpa Young said. "Jim was the

last, and Mamie here's my wife. She's not your child, Ma."

"Well, no matter. She's been long in the house. She's a good girl, but a little contrary." The old woman looked wonderingly at Phyllis, making in her throat those troubled sounds she always made when her mind clouded again after a clear moment. "And who are you, child?" she asked. "I seem to remember you. Did you have a baby? You look young to be a mother. Why, you look like a young girl, and your hand is so soft. Aren't you the one has a little baby?"

"Not until spring, Gran'ma," Phyllis said, and stroked with her free hand the old hands that held hers.

"Well, then we've no business to talk like we been. We've no business to talk of death and hard times and trouble in front of you. This is one to be cherished, Son. You tell whichever of the boys' she is, Arch. She's not hardy."

Arch leaned toward his mother and put his hand on her shoulder. "It's Christmas Day, Ma!" he yelled. "Today is Christmas!"

"Oh yes, so they said," old Grandma said. "I woke in my own bed. And are there bells? In Indiana there were always bells. We'd hear them of a morning. They had seven churches in that town, and one would have served. Clear out in the country like we were, clear out to my pa's place, we could hear the bells, clear out to the mill. Open the windows, Arch. Let's hear them. Silas and I, we'd lean out the window. He was a fine boy. Cheeks like apples. Open the windows, Son."

"That's a good idea. It's warm in here," Mamma Young said. "Let's open the window, Phyllis. You look sick, child. Are you all right?"

"How far along is she?" old Grandma asked. "Two and a half months, I always said, is the hard time to get by. If you're going to miscarry you're most like to miscarry at two and a half months. I carried every one of my nine full time, myself. But I remember my Aunt Kate used to say—"

"It's stuck a little, with the frost, I guess," Mamma Young said, working with the window. Phyllis helped her. When the window went up, old Grandma from over by the stove breathed in as deeply as she could of the snowy air. "Good; good," she said.

Cleo had come from upstairs and was standing, still in her pyjama jacket, still with her hair uncombed, looking at the tree.

"Did you have a good sleep?" Phyllis asked her.

92

"Did you get your sleep out?"

"Yes," Cleo said. Her eyes were very wide, very disappointed. "I sent away," she said in a high complaining voice, "I sent away and borrowed money and got Harvey a present, and he's not opened it. It's still here on the tree. I got him a present and Betty some dishes."

"She loves the dishes," Phyllis said. "She's played with them a lot this morning. Harvey didn't see your present, I guess. He'll find it when they come in. They're down on the river, skating."

"He can go to hell," Cleo said, and went, sobbing, into her room.

"Oh dear," Mamma Young said, "what's to be done? I try, but I don't know what to do for the girl. Should I go to her?"

"Leave her be," old Grandma said. "You leave her be, Mamie. She's a stranger. That's all she is. George should have let the missionaries keep her. George meant well, I'm sure, but it was a mistake. George had the kindest heart in the family, but he was so headstrong. Bullheaded, really."

"Come to the window," Phyllis said. "Come see them, Gran'ma Young. The men are coming. Come see, Betty. Daddy's coming, and all of them."

Mamma Young came and little Betty, but old

Grandma, if she heard, preferred to stay by the stove.

"One, two, three; four, five, six!" Betty counted.

"How black they look in the snow!" Phyllis said. It was snowing so hard they could not see the fences. The three tall figures and the three small ones stood out sharply in the moving whiteness.

"You mustn't catch cold," Mamma Young said to Phyllis. She drew her apron up around the girl's shoulders. "I think you've been a little feverish the whole morning. There's fever in your face. And your hair's full of snow."

"Well, are the bells ringing?" old Grandma croaked. "If they're not, how'd you like to put down that window? You're chilling me to the bone. You seem to forget, Mamie, I'm an old woman."

Mamma Young drew Phyllis away and put down the window. "Now, what'll we *do* with 'em, all over the house until dinner's on the table?" she asked. "They'll take the place. Edna'll be so cross."

"Send 'em out to cut wood," old Grandma said. "That's what my pa used to say; but *there,* acourse we had the wood, in Indiana, and here we haven't. I can't get used to burning these cobs, no, not all the time I've lived in this country. A cob fire's a puny thing. True, when we came, there was noth-

94

ing to burn but cow-chips and buffalo-chips, and we were glad enough to have 'em. But I used to say to Pa, more than anything, more than things to do with, round the house, I missed a good wood fire. It wasn't a thing you'd know about ahead and get set to do without either. I came, but I think, if I'd known there'd be nothing fit to burn, I'd've stayed. Law me, those winters, and Christmas come, there wasn't anything to it, but the day itself."

Little Betty came and leaned against her great-grandmother's side. She stood on tiptoe and put her mouth against the old woman's ear. "*Did* they, Gran'ma Young?" she whispered. "Did those angels sing: 'Glory to God'?"

"Why, acourse!" old Grandma said. "Don't anybody read this child the Bible? Why, yes, of course! 'The glory of the Lord shone round about them.' That's what they sang, and 'Peace on Earth!'"

"Shall we go help Edna?" Phyllis asked Betty, and reached for the child's hand.

Ralph met them in the doorway, caught up his girl and swung her high, and then rubbed his cold cheek against her neck. "Well, Pet," he said, "you having a good Christmas? Holy mackerel! All those presents *yours*? What are you going to call your doll?"

"Marjorie, I guess," Betty said.

"Wish you'd gone along, Phyllis. How are you?"

"I'm fine," Phyllis said. "Only I feel a little giddy. I've felt a little giddy all morning."

"Well, you look all right. You look swell. Where'd you get that dress? I never saw this one before, did I?"

"Not very likely. I've only *had* it since before we were married."

"You don't say! Well—I guess you never wore it, then."

A whining cry came from the kitchen, and Phyllis drew away and looked at him searchingly, her lips tight-set. "Those boys are teasing Betty again," she said.

"Well, now, keep your shirt on, honey. Don't get excited. They won't kill her. I'll go out there and see to them. It's Christmas, you know." There was tenderness under his mocking tone.

She leaned to him and he bent to kiss her mouth. "Merry Christmas, Baby!" he said.

Beyond the safeness and strength of his touch Phyllis felt the whole house and the difference that was on it because of the day.

"Christmas *is* something," she said. "And thank you for the mirror. It's lovely."

Edna came by them with a heavy dish in her hand. She set the dish down on the table and stepped over by the tree and for an instant leaned above Betty's little table and looked down into the gift-mirror that was lying there. Then she moved heavily into the kitchen. In the instant of the door-swing Phyllis heard her mother-in-law singing clearly, above the sound of a cream-whip in the bowl: "All the bells on earth shall ring on Christmas Day in the morning!"

SPRING:

PHYLLIS put out her hand to pick up her comb from the dresser. When her fingers slid over bare wood and left their mark she saw that it was only the outline of the comb where it had lain in the dust, the night. She had forgotten in her sleepiness that she had already picked it up and put it on the candy-box which held her embroidery threads.

Little Betty had gone from her own bed to her parents' and was sitting astride her father's chest chanting: "Daddy, you're a big old, rocky old hill, with the old dirt all blown away! What am I?"

"You're a darn nuisance," Ralph said fondly, yawned, and set his teeth lightly on the little knee against his face.

"You're not a *bear*!" Betty squealed; "you're a hill, Daddy!"

Phyllis peered into the little wavy mirror over the dresser and said: "Ralph, I'm gray. I've got two gray hairs. Or maybe it's just the dust. My hair's gritty."

Ralph laughed in his throat and held Betty's pommeling fists away from him. "How is it?" he asked. "Looks clearer to me!"

Phyllis resolved in her heart not to hold Ralph's indifference to her first gray hairs against him and moved heavily to the little window.

"It's fine," she said. "So still. And I can see clear to the cottonwoods."

Little Betty stopped tussling with her father, slid from the bed, and went to the window to see for herself. Phyllis thought her little figure, shadowed under her gown against the window, distressingly thin. She wished so that the child would eat more and be less restless. If only Edna's boys would leave the girl alone! For a week, because of the dust, the school had been closed and the boys, shut up in the house, had been noisy and meaner than ever. Betty

99

dreaded their teasing and tagged her grandmother about the place all day and cried if one of the boys pointed a finger at her. Phyllis decided that when school began again, she would keep Betty at home, teach her herself, and give the child a chance to be carefree and happy for at least part of the daylight hours.

"Get dressed, Betty," she said. "It's almost breakfast time. Your Aunt Edna's been downstairs a long time."

"*Aunt* Edna?" Betty said. "Is Edna my aunt? I didn't know Edna was my aunt. *Is* she, Daddy?"

Ralph was sitting on the edge of the bed, putting on his socks. " 'Fraid so, Pet," he said, and grinned at Phyllis over his child's head. "We hadn't meant to tell you until you were much older, until you had all your second teeth at least," he said in a deep-down voice that Betty knew at once for his foolishness voice. She laughed expectantly. "But since you've asked, Edna is your aunt in a way, and Cleo is another, and no help for it."

Phyllis smiled, pleased to see him in such a good mood. "Shame on you, Ralph!" she said, and drew Betty to her and fastened the child's underwaist. "Uncle Tom married Aunt Edna, and Uncle Harvey married Cleo, and so they're your aunts," she explained.

Betty, who until that moment had thought that marriages came only to princesses and princes and never certainly to one's own uncles, nodded gravely.

Ralph set his arms akimbo and sang in his deepest bass: "And they all lived together in a little crooked house."

When they had gone downstairs, Betty on Ralph's shoulder, Phyllis went slowly about the room, putting it to rights. She made up her bed and Ralph's and the little box-on-two-chairs bed that was Betty's. There was a homy gayety about the room, once it was in order, that always surprised and comforted her much. The red-and-white quilts she and her mother-in-law had hung for curtains to shut off the storeroom part, the red-dotted, thin Swiss curtains at the window that had once been the voluminous skirt of her mother-in-law's Sunday summer dress, and the blue-and-white quilt on the big bed gave the unfinished low-raftered room color and life. And it was their own, hers and Ralph's and Betty's, away from the rest of the house and the Young family. Here Ralph was more himself than he ever was downstairs, and here Betty, away from

101

her cousins' rough teasing, laughed and played and was a different child.

After she had dusted the window-ledge and the dresser and little rocking-chair, Phyllis sat on the edge of her bed resting. Breathing was very hard for her. She wondered how much easier it would be without the dust. She remembered that the last weeks before Betty's birth had been long and trying ones. But there was no comparison between that time and the present. That had been a wet and lovely spring, with the fields green as far as she could see from her window, and the mornings sweet with lark song. She would wake in the big maple bed to hear Olga, her noisy, big-hearted hired girl, moving about the house. Ralph would come in from the morning chores, smelling of the stable, hang his hat on the bedpost, give it a whirl, and say: "How are you, Baby? Don't get up unless you feel like it." Ralph had begun to call her "Baby" in fun during the months of their engagement, and the name had rooted. How she had been cherished!

Below stairs the life of the house was in noisy motion. Edna was doubtless getting breakfast with Mamma Young's help. Already Mamma Young's voice was raised breathily in a hymn: "Peace, peace, sweet peace; wonderful gift from above . . ." Old Grandma Young would be sitting up in her bed in the kitchen corner, having her say about the weather, assuring anybody who would listen that she'd seen as bad dust-storms in the old days when they lived in the sod house, and that the grasshoppers were a "good sight worse" anyway, grumbling a little at not finding herself in the room that had been hers for almost half her long life. Cleo would still be sleeping in old Grandma's room, and the kitchen would be free of menfolk. Edna's three boys were in the house; their shouting and scuffling came up faintly.

Phyllis heard slow, heavy steps on the stairs, and knew her mother-in-law was coming up to see how she was. "Hoo-hoo," the old woman said at the door, and came in with her rolling, comfortable walk. "Well, how do you feel?" she asked, and sat down by Phyllis and laid a plump warm hand on her knee. "Little better, with the wind down, isn't it?"

"Much," Phyllis said. "Is breakfast ready?"

"Almost. The menfolks are just coming in. But don't come down if you don't feel up to it. I'll fix a plate for you and send you up some coffee."

The Home Place: SPRING

"I'll go down," Phyllis said. "It spoils Edna's day if I don't come down." She laughed and sat gasping after her laugh.

"Well, never mind her," Mamma Young said. "She's got Cleo to fret about now. I must say, myself, I don't know how Cleo sleeps so late. How do you suppose she ever managed when she had to get up and go to an office of a morning? It was ten when she got to the kitchen yesterday morning, and she wasn't dressed then. I wish you'd seen Edna. She didn't *say* anything, didn't even look at her; but my! And Edna's washing this morning. I put your wash in with the rest. And it's a *wash*, I tell you. Over two weeks—now if the wind'll only stay down till it dries. The first boiler of white clothes is on now. Cleo'll have to do her own wash by hand, I guess. I went in and got Harvey's shirts and underthings and she never woke. My, the good shirts that boy has—enough to do all our boys for Sunday for years, and they're wearing out so fast, wearing them in the field. Next time we've any cash on hand I'm going to buy up a whole bolt of shirting and make a lot of shirts. My, the shirts I used to make when the three boys were all home, and the washings we'd have. Sometimes three lines full and the yard fence

104

too, with just the men's clothes. And still I wished I had a girl to sew for."

"Let's go down," Phyllis said, and they went down together, Mamma Young a step ahead, turning to put up a steadying hand, saying: "Take it easy on these stairs. I declare, I don't know how Arch ever got by both his mother and me and built in such steep old stairs. I guess he thought we'd never be using the upstairs much. Oh, dear!" Mamma Young finished most of her recollections of other years with a tender, forgiving "Oh, dear!"

"It's funny," Phyllis said, "how you always feel without thinking that when you go downstairs, or when you go up, if you're down, that the air will be easier to breathe there."

"Well, the kitchen's full of steam from the washing, and if that's not easier to breathe it's different, anyway."

In the kitchen Phyllis went at once to her husband's old grandmother and sat down on the bed beside her. It was best to get the old woman's warnings and omens about the weather and the family health out of the way first thing. Old Grandma, confused as she was about almost everything, always remembered that Phyllis was the one of her grandsons' wives that was soon to have a baby. She always had ready some piece of advice, dipping back into her memory, bringing up scraps of woman-wisdom from even before her own time. "There's a herb," she told Phyllis quaveringly, "grows down beyond the mill. I've heard my Aunt Kate speak of it. You take a path, she says, and go down beyond the oaks and there 'tis—a round-leafed plant. Boil it and drink the water off it. Keeps the feet and ankles from swelling. In Indiana, the folks' place in Indiana, you go down beyond the mill. You take a path . . ." Old Grandma lost herself, along the path back in Indiana, and slowly let go Phyllis's hands, shut her eyes, and swallowed loudly in her corded throat.

The menfolk were washing and combing and getting ready for breakfast.

"Mighty fine day," Grandpa Young was saying loudly, so that his old mother, who loved weather as she loved her life, might hear and be glad. "Clearest day we've had for a month. Pity it's not a school day, Betty. Think they'd have school, clear as it is, if it wasn't Saturday."

Edna was filling oatmeal bowls with thick oatmeal, and little Betty, pleased and important, was carrying them to the table for her, saying: "There!"

as she put down each bowl, just as her grandmother said "There." Grandpa saw and winked at Ralph, pleased as he always was with Betty's ways. He moved to his place at the head of the long table, sat down, and looked round on his sons and his sons' wives and his grandchildren. "All here, Mamma?" he asked. "Looks like we can work today, boys. A fine day." He bowed his head and said the blessing. Edna got up as soon as he had finished and brought the coffee. Only Cleo's place was vacant. Mamma Young had insisted, despite her protests, that old Grandma should not get up, because she had had two dizzy spells the day before. The old lady ate noisily, propped against her pillow, wanting them at the table not to forget her.

"Who's missing?" Grandpa Young asked innocently, noticing Cleo's unturned plate. "Somebody sick?"

"Who do you suppose?" Edna said.

The older boys, Tom and Ralph, knew well that Grandpa had not thought of making trouble, that he was as free from guile as a man could be; but Harvey, who was less used to his father's ways since his return, felt reproached and got up and said: "I'll fetch her," and went into the dining-room and on to old Grandma's room to wake his wife.

107

"Now here," Grandpa called, "that's all right. Never mind, Son." He puckered his mouth to whistle, as he always did when he was embarrassed, and then remembered he was at table and took a long whistling drink of coffee instead and sighed.

"Edna is my aunt," Betty announced cheerfully, "and so is Cleo!"

Her cousins laughed loudly, and little George said: "Aw, you crazy, didn't you know *that*?"

Cleo came in with Harvey, her yellow hair in a knot on the back of her head, washed, and came to the table. She wrapped her pyjama jacket tightly about her, hunched her shoulders, and said: "No, thanks," shortly when her father-in-law passed her the cream pitcher, and pushed the oatmeal bowl from her with the palm of her hand. She sipped her coffee slowly and spoke to no one.

Grandpa outlined the work for the day, finishing with a kind: "If that suits you, boys." He was happy that a day had come fit for work. Phyllis thought he was disappointed that his sons were so silent and unresponsive.

Tommy, Edna's oldest boy, shouted for more oatmeal, and Edna reached across the table and handed him Cleo's bowl. "Here," she said, "oatmeal's not good enough for some people." Cleo put up her thin red-nailed hands and pressed the pins tighter in the knot of her hair. "I said I wasn't hungry," she said. "I can't eat when I'm dragged out this early in the morning. I've *told* you I don't want breakfast." She set her teeth on her under lip and looked across the table at Tom, a wide-eyed, direct, hurt look. Tom looked down quickly and said: "Bread, please, Mamma," and did not look up again.

Cleo pushed her chair back from the table, wound her bare feet in mules about the rungs, breathed on her nails, and rubbed them on the worn brocaded lapel of her pyjama jacket.

Phyllis and her mother-in-law exchanged one of their brief communing glances. Harvey saw it, and said: "Cleo, for Pete's sake, do you have to do your nails at the table?"

"Why, I'm not doing my nails," Cleo cried in her high voice. "I was just looking at them. My God, I can't do a *thing*, you don't bark at me. The whole bunch of you! You think just because—"

"Oh, keep still," Harvey said. "Go get some clothes on and quit this 'poor little me'!"

Tom looked up at Harvey, opened his mouth to speak, decided against it, reached out and clamped a hand on his youngest son's shoulder, and said: "What's your hurry? You don't need to take bites like that, do you?"

Cleo got up from her place and said: "I don't do a thing! You come in and drag me out here before I can fix my hair even, and then jump on me 'cause I'm not dressed. Whata you want? I can't do a thing you aren't all over me!" Her voice had risen to a scream. Old Grandma in her bed said loudly: "George, George, who is this woman? What's she doing here?"

Ralph, who had a way with his old grandmother, went to her and explained gently: "That's *Harve*, Gran'ma, not George. That's Harve's wife."

"Oh," the old lady said, "that's right. I forgot. Come here, child," and held out her hand. Cleo went to her and sat down on the edge of the bed, fumbled in her jacket pocket for a cigarette, lighted it, and flipped the match toward the cob-box.

Harvey looked round on his family, ashamed as he always was for Cleo's smoking. When they first came home he had forbidden her to smoke after he saw the horror in his mother's face, but Cleo had cried and been unmanageably bitter. "Are you *crazy?*" she had wailed. "Just because we've got to live off here in the sticks with this outfit, do we have to *act* like 'em?"

"Well," old Grandma had soothed her daughter-in-law, "my Aunt Kate smoked a pipe and she lived to ninety-four. I can stand that a lot better'n I can the way she fixes up. I never thought George'd go off up there and bring home a heathen woman." A whole winter's association with Harvey and Cleo had not convinced old Grandma that Harvey was not her son George.

Old Grandma took Cleo's hand in hers, looked at the red nails, and said: "Weren't there any missionaries up there, George? Couldn't you learn her something yourself?"

"Precious little," Harvey said loudly. Cleo jerked her hand from old Grandma's and ran into her room. Harvey took his hat and followed his brother Tom from the kitchen.

Phyllis went to the door with Ralph. He kissed her and said: "Get outside, Baby, why don't you? While it's nice like this."

"Yes," his mother said, "come with me, Phyllis. I'm going to set out plants until Edna has the clothes ready to hang out. A day like this puts some hope in a body."

"Is it going to rain?" Betty cried. "Is it, Gran'pa?"

"Bless you, it don't look it," Grandpa said, and put his hand on her curls. "But it's still and clear and sunny. It's the best day we've had."

When the menfolks and the little boys had gone, Phyllis gathered up the dishes. "I'll do them," she told Edna; "you go on with your washing. No telling how long it'll stay clear like this."

Edna gave her short snort of a laugh. "Better keep off your feet," she said. "Leave the dishes till I get the wash out. I'll do them then."

"No, I'll wash them," Phyllis said, and Edna made no more protest, but went back to her washing-machine. Phyllis felt that her mother-in-law was right, that Edna's hatred for Cleo had pretty well crowded out her grudge toward Phyllis. When Edna stopped her washing, dried her hands, and took the heavy platter from Phyllis to set it up on the high pantry shelf, Phyllis felt something near to kindness in her: "Here, let me do that!"

When she had finished with the dishes, Phyllis decided to sew a while and went to old Grandma's room, that had been hers and Ralph's room when they first came to the home place, to get some pillow-slips from a trunk that was still there. She thought she might make the pillow-slips over into baby clothes, into a dress and underskirt to match, for the new baby. When she rapped at the door, Cleo said: "Who is it?" and then: "Come in."

Cleo was lying on the unmade bed. "I'm sorry to bother you," Phyllis said, trying not to look at the disorder, "but I want some things from my trunk."

"Okay, go ahead," Cleo said.

Phyllis opened up her trunk and began laying piles of towels and pillow-cases on the old sofa.

"You sure have stuff enough," Cleo observed. "You didn't make it all yourself, did you?"

"Most of it," Phyllis said. "The girls in my building gave me a shower too. I was teaching then, you know."

"Yes, Harvey said you were a school-teacher. I don't see how you could do it. I'd never have the patience, myself. Kids drive me nuts."

Phyllis said nothing.

"Most of them do," Cleo said. "Yours is cute. But those boys! Aren't they just the meanest, orneriest little devils you ever saw?"

"Yes!" Phyllis said from a pent-up heart. "Yes, they are."

"It's not Tom's fault," Cleo went on quickly. "*He's* all right, Tom is. But what can he do? It's *hers!*"

Phyllis was silent. To concur in Cleo's opinion of Edna's boys was one thing. To touch on the very sore subject of Edna's behavior was another. Cleo was looking at her keenly, eagerly.

"There's little any of us can do," Phyllis said. "We're here. We've lost our homes. The folks are doing their best to make us at home here. We'll just have to wait and—" She recognized her voice as her old school-teaching one, and stopped.

"And *what*?" Cleo shrilled. "It's not so bad for you. They *like* you; they all carry you round on a chip, and Ralph's swell to you. What would you do if he ever lit into you the way Harve lights into me every time I open my mouth, when I'm not doing a *thing*? He's jealous. That's what. He's jealous of Tom just because he's treated me decent. The whole bunch of them are down on me. Are we all just gonna stay on here? Why don't they *do* something?"

"Maybe we can get out, maybe we can find something a little later," Phyllis said, her voice trembling. "But, you see, Tom and Ralph are farmers. They had their own places. They want to farm again." She spread out her hands. "When things are better, when it rains—when this clears up—here the land isn't spoiled like it is out west. When it rains—"

"What, when it rains?" Cleo cried. "We'll still *be*

here. Can a little old place like this keep a dozen people? Why don't Harve get out and find something? I tell you what, he's not trying. He thinks if he stays here he'll break me, that I'll get out, leave him. See?"

"Oh, dear!" Phyllis said, like her mother-in-law.

"Well, maybe I will. He's asking for it. Let him take what he gets."

"He's asked for what?" Phyllis asked.

"He'll see," Cleo said, and selected the longest of the cigarette-ends in the saucer on the chair by the bed and put it into her holder.

Phyllis put the pillow-cases back in the trunk—she had decided she could not sew that morning. She went out to where her mother-in-law and little Betty were setting out pansy plants beside the house.

"My goodness, child, you're white!" Mamma Young said. "What you been doing?"

"Talking with Cleo," Phyllis said.

She could indeed see "clear to the cottonwoods." The sun, that for so many days had been what old Grandma called "end-of-the-world red," was a paler color. "I think I'll go for a walk," she said. "I think I'll walk to the cottonwoods."

"Oh, do you think you ought to?" Mamma Young said, straightening up with a hand on her back.

115

"That's quite a piece. You better take Betty with you."

But Betty did not want to go. To be setting out plants with her grandmother was a lot more fun than walking to the cottonwoods with her mother. Phyllis did not urge her. She really wanted to go alone. Inside the fence she walked slowly in the brittle grass, watching the little puffs of dust that rose with each step. It was spring, but the earth and the young grass and the air smelled not of life but of death. If she could do without breathing it would not be half so bad; but to be conscious, painfully conscious, of each breath was trying, saddening. When she came to the top of the gently rolling hill she could look down on the dry drifted creek-bed and see where the sod house had stood when old Grandma Young had come out from Indiana. The great cottonwoods were of Young planting. She came to the first of the trees and rested, standing panting, with her back against it. She went on to the biggest tree, sat down, leaning against it, and looked up into the maze of its little dusty, gray-green leaves.

From where she sat she could see the Young home place, with the little figures of Mamma Young and Betty moving between the well and the flower-garden. Across the road from the Young place the big square house Tom had built for Edna stood up against the roiled sky. Phyllis disliked the house with a shamed, rebellious dislike. It was ugly, stolid, like Edna. It stood for Tom's and Edna's unjust feeling that Ralph and she, because Tom and his father had helped Ralph buy land and farm machinery that had had to go, were to blame more than anyone or anything else for the anxious poverty they all lived in now.

The little old Young house was prettier than most, with its vines and porches and gateways. Mamma Young's seal was on it. It looked peaceful, clean, and good. There were only two people in it, as she looked on, Phyllis reminded herself—two un-loved, bitter women. One was working in a steamy kitchen, the other was lying on her bed in a dis-ordered room or standing before old Grandma's speckled mirror, coaxing a wave into her yellow hair or thinning her eyebrows with a pair of tweez-ers. Maybe Cleo would make her threat good. Maybe she would "do something." Maybe she would go away.

A car stopped on the highway and a woman leaned

117

out to shout: "Anything wrong?" It was strange no doubt to see a woman sitting under the cottonwoods alone in the forenoon.

"No, thank you. No," Phyllis shouted back, her hands cupped around her mouth. The car moved on.

Phyllis got up and began gathering tumbleweeds from along the fence, to pile them together and make a little hiding-place for herself. She skewered the weeds together with sticks she picked up and a couple of dried cornstalks. Her bower hid her from the road and left the field and house in clear view. She took off her sweater, rolled it to use for a pillow, and lay down. Lying there, the land seemed wider, kinder. She went to sleep, and an ant, crawling on her arm, woke her. Below her in the field a little whirlwind played by itself. Down near the dry creek-bed she saw something moving, and as they came nearer, she made out a pheasant cock and three hens going their slow and rhythmic way. They were not shining, superb, as pheasants ought to be. They were dull, bedraggled, and scrawny. The sight of them made her sadder than anything she had known during the winter. She had thought herself immune from any but duller sorrows, but the ruined pheasants made her cry with sudden, hurting sobs. When she looked again, the birds were

still in sight, taking their slow way down the creek-
bed. She went to sleep and slept fitfully, dimly conscious of the rough ground under her and of the
ant that had come to travel along her arm again.

The wind woke her with its strong smell of pow-
dered furrows.

She got to her feet and leaned against the tree
a minute, looking toward the house. There a little
Edna was scurrying along, taking in her clothes
from the line. The whipping bit of pink would be
her own apron. Dust rose in whirls from the field

and hid the house. She saw that she had better start for home. If a bad wind came she might lose her way and they would be anxious about her. She kept close to the fence as she went, took off her sweater and put it over her head, and walked as fast as she could. She had watched so many dust-storms, from the little window in the ell room, from the kitchen downstairs, but she had never been out in one for longer than it took her to walk from the yard into the house. She was excited and frightened. The wind came in only infrequent gusts and the going was unpleasant, nothing worse. But the hurrying was too much for her. She stopped and rested against a fence-post. Her sweater sleeve caught on a barb of the fence-wire and she struggled to get it loose, her eyes almost shut against the sifting cloud, when she heard someone calling her name and saw one of the men running up the slope toward her. It was not Ralph, but Tom.

"Hi, there," he panted. "Mamma's scared stiff about you. How far'd you go?"

She tried to answer him and found that she hadn't the breath for it.

"I don't think it's going to blow bad," he said. "It's no storm, just a little wind. You take it easy. If it blows hard, I'll carry you." She took his arm and hurried along beside him, head down, the sweater over her face, and stopped for breath whenever she felt she could go no farther without resting.

Ralph came to meet them when they were resting a moment on the last rise, and scolded with loving anger. "Good Lord, Baby, why'd you go so far? I didn't know you'd gone. Came in—put up the team —didn't know till I got to the house. . . ." He had been running and was out of breath.

Before she could answer him Tom had gone on, leaving Ralph to look after her. When they reached the yard gate Grandpa was there to open it and add his word of concern. Mamma Young, with Betty clinging to her apron, was on the step to meet them.

Old Grandma was out of her bed, insisting loudly that they should send for the doctor, that Phyllis would be sure to have her baby "right away," and Edna said: "Well, she's here and she seems all right. How'd it be to eat dinner before it's stone cold?"

Mamma Young insisted that Phyllis should go to bed and rest. Ralph went upstairs with her, and his mother came up almost at once with a large pan of warm water, soap, and a towel. "Go on down, Son, and get your dinner," she said to Ralph. "I'll see to Phyllis."

Mamma Young knelt and took off Phyllis's shoes

and stockings, talking soothingly all the while.

In bed, after her bath and a bowl of hot potato soup, Phyllis fell asleep almost at once, with her mother-in-law's voice droning on gently. She was dreaming that she was in her father's house, and that he had just come home from his office at the bank and was saying: "Got something for my girl. Guess what!" and that he had taken from under his coat one of her embroidered pillow-slips and handed it to her like a sack. Inside the sack she had felt the little body of a newborn baby stirring. "Oh, it's come," she thought, "with no fuss, no pain, no worry." Her father had seen to everything in his quiet kindly way. Someone was knocking, and she ran to the door and peeked out to see if it might be Ralph, and sure enough it was Ralph. "Ralph," she called, eager to tell him that the baby had come with no bother to anyone—and woke to hear Harvey saying: "It's Harve. May I come in?"

She sat up in bed and drew the quilt up under her chin.

"Come in," she said. "Is it night already?"

Harvey sat down in the little rocker. "No, just getting a little thicker," he said. "Sure is dark up here. Shall I light a lamp?"

"Please do," Phyllis said. "There on the dresser."

When the lamp was lighted, Harvey looked about the room and said: "Well, I declare—as Mamma says —you've certainly worked this place over. Best-looking room in the house."

"Thanks," Phyllis said. "It's your mother's quilts make it so cozy. I think when I have a house again, I'll hang quilts for curtains all over the place."

"Is all the junk that used to be stored up here behind those red-and-white ones?" Harvey asked. "Care if I look?"

She listened to his rummaging about while the lamp he carried threw his shadow on the rafters. He came back presently, set the lamp down on the floor, and said: "Will you look at this now! My knife. Tom gave me this knife. Must have been when I was eight or ten. Tom's quite a bit older than Ralph and me, you know; couple of boys between him and Ralph that died when they were little." He opened the blades and laid the knife in his palm, blades up, and held it out for Phyllis to admire. "This is a good knife," he said, turning it back in the lamplight. "Boy! I remember when I lost it and hunted everywhere for it. I got down and rolled over the whole yard—when you lose a knife in the grass, the only way to find it is to roll for it. I remember I used to lie in bed and try to remember where I had it last.

123

That old train that goes by around nine used to have the longest, saddest old wail of a whistle; well, it used to say one thing to me—I'd hear it over the bluffs by the river—'I lo-o-o-st it right along h-e-e-re somewhere. . . .' Mamma must have found it some place and put it away for me up here." He sat down on the floor and began to play mumblety-peg with the knife. He sighed. "Yes, sir," he said, "Tom gave me this knife. Never thought then I'd be stalking my wife to keep her from working on him, did I?"

"What?" Phyllis asked. That Tom watched Cleo, knew always when she came into the room and where she was in the room and what she was doing, and that Cleo showed off for Tom, pouting and looking lonely and lost and abused, Phyllis knew well enough, and all the others knew; but nothing had ever been said about it.

"Right," Harvey said. "Cleo said she was going upstairs to look out the south window and see if it was clearing up any, and almost right away Tom says he's going up after his watch. So—up I go. They've just gone down. I've been doing that sort of trailing the best part of the winter, in a quiet brotherly way. Don't know why I bother."

Phyllis looked at him. The lamp lighted his face

clearly. There was nothing in his expression to suggest any deeper concern than his words suggested.

"I don't think—" Phyllis began.

"That anything will come of it? No, I suppose not. He'll just go on mooning and pulling his long face and being the devil to get on with when we're out working. No, siree! We were fearfully and wonderfully brought up, we Young boys. I can't see any of us going in for adultery." He tossed the knife farther than he had tossed it before and left it standing in the board until it stopped quivering before he reached for it.

"Oh Lord," he said, "what I'd like would be some golf. That's one thing. I've still got my sticks. I left 'em out there and never went back after 'em. We could lay out a few holes along the creek. Met my best girl, playing golf."

"I wouldn't think of Cleo playing," Phyllis said, sure that Harvey was not speaking of Cleo.

"Cleo? I guess not. No. No, this girl's name was Doris. I used to go out to her brother's place to play. She came to visit. I was out there a lot. About every week-end."

"What happened?"

"Nothing. I couldn't have bought her shoes."

"Her shoes likely didn't mean a lot to her. You

125

should have asked her anyway."

"Maybe. I didn't think so at the time. She was married last fall. A real nice wedding. Took up a whole page in the *Tribune*."

"And so you married Cleo?" Phyllis said.

"Well, not just 'and so.' Cleo and I worked in the same place. You see, she took most of my dictation when I was in the office. I saw her a lot; she was up at my place a lot. She got mad about the time I met Doris. She had a chance to get another job. It wasn't as good salary, but it was easier, and it looked like it might amount to something more than the one she had. Well, she'd been mad and she came and asked me if I thought she ought to change—take this other job. I thought maybe she wanted to get out because we'd not been getting on very well, see, and I thought we could get on all right, and I didn't want her changing on my account, and I said I thought she ought to stay on. She'd been there longer than I had. I thought we could get on all right. Well, when this outfit went under we were both out of a job. I had my rent paid ahead, another month, on my apartment, and I was pretty sure I could get something to do—this was just before Doris was married. Cleo was pretty low. She owed some money for clothes and was behind with her rent." He

126

sighed again. "About a third of her stuff was over at my place anyway. We got married."

Phyllis remembered Harvey as he had looked at the time of her wedding. He was a junior in the University then. Her bridesmaids had been terribly awed at his good looks, his apparent sophistication, and his football record. Remembering her wedding, and looking at Harvey's face as he remembered his, brought tears to her eyes. "Will you hand me a handkerchief from the little blue box in the top dresser drawer, Harvey?" she asked.

"Right," he said. "I hope you didn't find my tale distressing. I'm pretty used to it myself." He lifted the lamp to the dresser and opened the drawer. "Say, who's this?" he asked, and took a picture from the drawer.

"Oh, that's an old sweetheart of Tom's. Your mother found it, when she was sorting the things in this room before I moved in. Isn't she pretty? I saved the picture out, put it in my drawer. I like to think of her as one of the family."

"Oh, sure, I can remember her. She *was* mighty pretty. Mamma thought Tom would never get over it when she died. . . . That was during the war."

"Do you think," Phyllis asked cautiously, "that she looks anything like Cleo?"

Harvey considered, holding the picture at arm's length. "No, I wouldn't say so. She was light and small. That's all the resemblance I'd see." He gave the handkerchief to Phyllis and saw the tears on her lashes. "Aw, say," he said, alarmed, "don't you think about that stuff. I'll get on with Cleo now for as long as she'll get on with me. I'm not worried about it. And Tom—he's pretty much married himself; and Edna will take care of herself. Here, I'll read you something."

He got down to look at the books in the little case under the window, selected one, and wiped the dust from it with his sleeve. "Here," he said, "I'll read you some poetry."

He sat in the little rocker and rocked while he hunted for a poem he thought would cheer and please her. Phyllis watched him and listened to the wind. Outside, with the added darkness of the dust, the air was a heavy, ugly brown. The floor, the window-ledge, the quilt under her hands were coated with dust. Her palms were gritty.

"The rain has taught us nothing at all."

Harvey was reading in his slow, deep voice. She thought to herself the dust had taught her something in the beginning, but it had stayed too long, dinged its lesson over and over, every day, almost every hour, until it meant nothing at all but a kind of angry, hopeless inanity.

> *"The hawk that motionless above the hill*
> *In the pure sky*
> *Stands like a blackened planet,"*

She thought of the pheasants in the field and how she had cried for them . . .

> *"Seeing him shut his wings and fall*
> *Has taught us nothing at all.*
> *In the shadows of the hawk we feather our nests."*

"We feather our nests," she repeated after Harvey; "that's what we do, isn't it?" and recognized, in spite of her feeling, the teacherliness in her voice.

Harvey closed the book with a finger at the place.

"Yes. Well," he said, "I guess *you* do. But you're the only one. Think Tom or I'd get a lot of kick out of nesting, hawks or no hawks?"

"There's your mother," Phyllis said.

"Yes, there's Mother and Dad. They've got on."

"Finish it," Phyllis said.

"Yes," Harvey said, but did not begin at once; he rocked, looking at the black window; the book hung in his huge hands between his knees.

Someone came upstairs. It was Ralph with little Betty hung across his shoulder like a meal-sack. The child was laughing and squealing happily.

"Hello," Ralph said, and set his daughter down on his brother's knee. "Didn't know you were up here, Harve."

"He's been reading to me," Phyllis said.

Little Betty took the book and read silently to herself, spelling the words with her lips.

"Mamma wants to know if you want your supper sent up or if you feel like coming down," Ralph said.

"I'll go down," Phyllis said, "but, oh, I dread those stairs! Did you boys fall down them when you were little?"

"Constantly," Harvey said, "or as often as we got past Mamma and Gran'ma and got the stair door open."

Phyllis said she thought she ought to dress, but Ralph said: "No, don't bother. Supper is ready. Come like you are. Here's your robe." He knelt and held her slippers for her, then picked her up in his arms. "Carry the lamp, Harve," he said, "and you run ahead and open doors, Betty."

"Oh, Ralph; down those steep stairs!"

"Afraid?"

"A little. Let me down!"

"Nope. Go on, Harve. If I drop you, Harve here will pass me the lamp, catch you, and you'll never know what happened."

Betty ran ahead and cried for everyone to "Come see Daddy carry Mother downstairs."

Over the lamp, over Harve's head, Phyllis looked down into the steamy kitchen. The room was hung with indoor clothes-lines, heavy with shirts, house dresses, and overalls; for the dust had come before the colored clothes were hung out. It was like looking down into a tropical forest where all the trees and vines were denim blue. From near the stove Edna looked up at her, a dish of steaming food in her hands. Her heavy face was homely with sweat and fatigue. Edna's boys shouted excitedly to see Ralph carrying Phyllis, and Tom went to the table and drew out Phyllis's chair for her.

"You'd think there was a fire," Edna said wearily.

Old Grandma said she felt lots better and that if they made her stay in bed any longer she'd rot, that she was going to get up. Ralph folded a quilt from her bed and hung it over her chair for her. "Here you are, Gran'ma," he yelled in her better ear. "Here's your chair fixed up for you," and helped her up and led her to the table.

"Well, that's fine," Grandpa said. "Nice to have everyone up to the table." He looked round and saw that Cleo was missing and began his breathy embarrassed whistle. Harvey went to the dining-room door and called Cleo, but she did not answer.

"Everything's going to be cold again," Edna said.

"Can't you keep from harping on that?" Tom said hotly. "The wind's so bad she didn't hear, likely."

"Well, the rest of us manage to get here," Edna said. "Looks like when she never lifts a hand to get a meal—"

Mamma Young saw that trouble was dangerously near. "Edna's tired," she said, "and it's discouraging to get a meal and have to see it get cold." She smiled appealingly at her sons.

"You bet I'm tired," Edna said, looking hard at Tom. "If you'd done a two-weeks' wash for thirteen people, and half of it so dusty it's got to be done over again, you'd be tired too."

"Did your sleep rest you good?" Mamma Young asked Phyllis.

Edna looked angrily at Phyllis. "My Lord," she cried, her heavy voice trembling with weariness, "you'd think nobody'd ever had a baby before!"

She got up from her chair and went to the stove and yanked open the oven door.

Grandpa Young took advantage of the sudden stillness to bow his head and ask the blessing. As soon as the "Amen" was said, Mamma Young got up from the table and went to Edna. "Why, Edna," she asked in a gentle, scared whisper, "you aren't, you aren't—*that way*, are you?"

"No," Edna said loudly, "and a lot of difference it would make if I was! Can't you see me carried to the table in a bathrobe if I was?" She laughed shortly, her ugly snorting laugh, and slid a pan of biscuits onto a plate.

Harvey came back from the dining-room and went to his mother. "Mamma, do you know where Cleo is? She's not in there."

"Why, I don't know, Son; she must be around somewhere. She—"

Tom got up from his chair. "She's gone," he said. "She went to town with the Fergusons."

"What?" Grandpa Young said; "what'd you say, Tom?"

"She went to town with the Fergusons," Tom said again loudly. "She's going in to Omaha on the train tonight. How long do you think she was going to stand it, like it was here?" He looked angrily at them all, his lower lip thrust out.

"And where," Edna asked, "did she get the money to go to Omaha?"

"I gave it to her," Tom said.

"You would!" Edna cried. "You'd take cream money, money we needed for shoes for the boys, for everything. . . ." Extreme tiredness had loosened Edna's tongue as anger and bitterness alone never had.

"Here!" Grandpa Young said sternly, and brought his knife-handle down on the table. "What's going on here? You mean Harvey's wife's gone away? What about it, Harvey?"

"I don't know," Harvey said. "I don't know anything about it. Maybe she got a job."

"No," Tom said. "Guy Ferguson was by this morning and he said he was going in to meet the train tonight because his wife's mother's coming, and I told Cleo, and she said she'd go with him. She means to get a job in Omaha. She'll stay there till she does."

"Well," Grandpa said, "I guess none of our womenfolks need to go out job-hunting. I guess we still have a roof. Mamma, did you know anything about this?"

"No, Arch, no, I didn't," Mamma Young said. "I

134

knew she was restless, but I didn't know she was planning to go away."

"How much did you give her?" Edna asked.

Tom did not answer.

"I heard the front door close a while ago," Mamma Young said, "but I just supposed it was one of the little boys going out that way."

"When'd she go?" Harvey asked.

"I don't know," Tom said. "She didn't say. I didn't know she *had* gone."

"Did Guy say he'd come by for her here?" Grandpa Young asked.

"No, she was going down the road to wait for him. He didn't know she's going."

"Then maybe she's not gone yet," Grandpa said. "Maybe she's down at the drive yet. Better go down, Harvey, hadn't you? Pretty mean night to be out in."

Harvey moved toward the door. Old Grandma put out her hands and caught at his sleeve. "What's going on? What's going on here?" she said shrilly. "George, who *is* it's gone? Is it your woman? Well, Son, you listen to me. Let'r go. Just let'r go. If it's her, let'r go! She wasn't the woman for you. Nobody's blaming you. Son, let'r go!"

The kitchen door opened, letting in a gust of

dusty wind, and Cleo. She slammed the door and leaned against it, coughing. "Why, there she is now!" old Grandma piped. "Oh, well."

"What do you think you're up to?" Harvey asked loudly.

Cleo shook her yellow head and stood coughing. Mamma Young went to the sink, filled the wash-pan with warm water from the reservoir, and said: "Well, it's an awfully bad night to go to town anyway. Come have your supper, come wash and have your supper."

Cleo pushed her suitcase to one side with her foot. She looked at Tom. "You *told* them," she cried. "What'd you do that for? You let me go out and wait alone in that dirty cold wind an hour, and nobody coming. . . ."

Tom looked at her, color climbing his neck, but he did not answer.

"We didn't any of us know you'd gone," Mamma Young said. "If we'd known, and you'd been determined to go, Harvey'd gone down, waited with you." There was reproach under her gentleness.

"Wash your face and come eat your supper," Harvey said.

"Oh, you!" Cleo cried. "I'm through taking orders from you. What do you care what happens to

136

me? I've taken all I'm going to off you. I couldn't go tonight, but I'm going! I'm going tomorrow, and nothing'll stop me."

"Not on the cream money, you're not," Edna said.

"What do you know about my money?" Cleo said. "It's not yours, I guess."

"It's not Tom's to give," Edna said. "And it's a cinch you've done nothing to earn it."

137

"Oh, leave her alone," Tom said.

"*Me* leave her alone!" Edna cried in her heavy, harsh voice. "I can get her meals, and wash the sheets off her bed, when she'll get out of it, and see you make a fool of yourself over her in front of your family all winter, and when you give her the cream money—I can just leave her alone!"

Grandpa Young got up from his chair and lifted his hands and shook them, palms up, in front of him. "Children, children!" he said, "stop it! This's no way to do. Sit down, sit down, all of you. Sit down!"

Cleo, her eyes still rimmed with dusty tears, went to her place and Harvey went to his. Mamma Young went to her husband and stood beside him, twisting her hands in her apron.

"This is all wrong," Grandpa said. "There's no sense in it. We've worked all our lives, Mamma and I, and Grandma too, to make this place and keep it; to bring you boys up, the best we could, and get you started. Things've been bad, and that you've had hard luck and are here we're not blaming you, and you're welcome. Mamma and I've done our level best to make you feel welcome. We've had a bad, dry year and the worst spring I ever saw, and I don't know how it's going to be or if we'll have any crops at all, but we ain't destitute. We got this place and work to do when it's fit, and no sickness. We got canned stuff in the cellar, and nobody's gonna go hungry. I don't know what's gonna be, but one thing I *do* know—this is gonna stop, this feeling and contention, and back talk! What kind of men've you grown up to be? You look at one another, but look at yourselves. I gotta say you don't act like you're the men your uncles were!

"You got to cut it out. Look to your families and get on with your wives and children. We've never had it in this house, Mamma and me, all these years —this contention. Your women talking like that— running away to get jobs! It's a shame to this house. You got to cut it out. It's too hard on your mother."

"Arch," Mamma Young said, turned from them and put her apron over her face.

The room was quiet except for Cleo's coughing. One of Edna's boys, overcome with the surprise and shame and quietness of the moment, slid under the table and stifled his giggles in his mother's apron.

Little Betty got down from her chair, went to her father and climbed onto his lap, rested her head against him, and said: "There *is* fruit in the cellar, and strawberries." Her voice rose in a squeal of laughter on the word "strawberries."

"Strawberries!" old Grandma cried. "The best strawberries I ever ate we found one night when we were coming out here from Indiana. I can't for the life of me tell you what state it was in even, but I remember I got down from the wagon and there, squashed on the wheel, was berries. I called to one of the women and I said: 'Here's berries,' and we got pails and gathered till we were just *feeling* for them in the grass. Such berries! Arch—but that was before you were born, wasn't it? Well, there's no tame berries nowadays'll ever taste like a wild one."

Phyllis gave a gasping moan that she had been holding back all through Grandpa's talk, and old Grandma, who had to be yelled at about almost everything, heard her, and said: "*There*, Mamie, what did I tell you!" and Mamma Young went to Phyllis.

"You want to go upstairs, Baby?" Ralph asked anxiously.

"If you'd rather," Mamma Young said, "we'll fix my room for you, Phyllis, so you can be downstairs."

"Oh, no," Phyllis said. "I—I want to go—home!"

"I'll go over to Ferguson's if you think I should now, Mamma, to phone?" Tom said.

Edna went to the stove, built up the fire and filled the big tea-kettle.

Little Betty started to follow her mother when she went to the stair door with Ralph's arm about her, but her grandfather called her back and took her on his knee. "I'll tell you a story," he said, stroking her hair gently. "Tell you a thing that happened when I wasn't any bigger'n Tommy here."

"Well, Cleo," Harvey said, "looks like we better do the dishes."

"Dishes?" Cleo said. "Stand out there in that dirt an hour and come in here and wash dishes! I guess—"

Harvey pressed a thumb and finger either side her slender wrists, and said: "I guess *so*." He let go her hands. She pulled an unironed apron from the line above her and tied it about her very slender waist and began scraping plates. Harvey helped her gather them up. He looked over at his father, where the old man sat with his granddaughter on his knee, as though he wanted him to see that for the moment at least, though he was doing it without enthusiasm, he was ruling his wife without contention.

Phyllis paused to rest part way up the stair and looked down through avenues of drying clothes, on her little daughter, on Edna, busy putting kettles of water to heat. Her mother-in-law was going ahead with the lamp, ready to stay up the night, to make the hours of pain and waiting easier for her. Tom

141

had already gone, driving through the dust, to fetch the doctor.

"Arch," old Grandma was shouting, "which way's the wind from? Be nice, all right, if it'd rain tonight, wouldn't it?"

"It would," Grandpa said, "though there's nothing to warrant it. I was just startin' telling the children here about a storm I was out in, going for cows, when I was eight. It was just about this time of the year."

SUMMER: To wake to
the hardy hymn of hens and the far and sweet
lament of turtle-doves, to see the sky so deep a
blue beyond the little window gave Phyllis such
happiness she wanted to sing. She laughed to herself when the song that came to her lips was one
of her mother-in-law's hymns: "On the other side
of Jordan, In the green fields of Eden . . ."

She put out a sleep-weak hand and laid it on the
rounded blanket in the basket beside the bed. What
a good baby to sleep so late! Mamma Young said he
was the best baby she had ever seen, and old

143

Grandma said she had seen but two as good and both had been "taken under three." She raised herself on her elbow to look at him. He was lying with his fists up on either side of his head. He was "all Young," as old Grandma had said when he was first laid in her lap. "Shoulder'n thigh," she had crowed, "this boy's all Young. The girl's yours, Phyllis, but this one's a Young." Phyllis had been sure from the first that his eyes were going to be like *her* father's, but she had kept this to herself.

"Hello, Son," she whispered. "Happy birthday!" The baby tucked down his chin, opened one eye, closed it again, and yawned. "Four weeks old," Phyllis said. "Want a party? Want to have on a dress and have a party?" The hands moved in wider circles and the mouth puckered. Phyllis lifted him into the bed beside her.

"He's too lazy to eat," she told her mother-in-law when Mamma Young came upstairs to carry the baby down for her. Mamma Young sat down on the bed beside her and patted the baby and crooned: "Was him Gran'ma's big boy, was him? Why, he eats like a hand, seems to me. Such a big boy! He's got a whopper appetite. I believe he weighs more'n any my boys did, at his age. Archie, the one we lost when he was still a baby, he was a heavy baby, but he wasn't as solid-fleshed, seems to me, as this child. Arch would have liked it, I think, if we'd named the next baby after him, too, but you know I couldn't. A baby's a person, no matter if you don't have it but five months. I remember all his ways, clearer, I think, than I remember any of them when they were babies, except Harvey. The baby, you know, the last one, without another one on the way to get ready for and take care of when it comes, gets so much more looking after and notice. And the other children, the older ones, they all keep saying: 'Look at baby!' Now they're all grown, things are always reminding our boys, the older two, of things Harvey did and said when he was a baby. That helps you to remember things, I think. They made so much over Harvey, the older boys, Tom especially. He'd let that child tag him all over the place, or he'd carry him on his shoulder. Pick him up and hold him way up above his head, and the little fellow'd hold his knees stiff and spread out his arms and balance. He was such a strong little boy. Tom was so proud of him. Took more notice of him than he ever has of any of his own boys, really. He was the best brother.

"I worry about Harvey, Phyllis. The boy's restless, and he's getting a kind of grim way, and I hate to see it. He works, works right along with the other boys, but he works like he was hired here. He acts *homesick*, yes he does. Tom's at home here—of course, he's never been off the place—and Ralph's taken hold and made himself at home, but Harve's just holding down his restlessness. I don't think he's lonesome for the job he had and city ways and people and all that. When he used to come home on visits he was lonesome, restless, then. And it's not just Cleo. I think he knew pretty much what she was when he married her. And a man's a lot more practical, nearly always, about however a marriage turns out, than a woman is. I guess we led him to expect too much, Arch and me and the boys, when he was in school and everything made easy for him, everything coming his way. It led him on so to expect something extra that's not come, and he feels let down. Oh, if you'd seen him, Phyllis, just out of high school; he was so tall and hardy, and he had such an open, clear look, so ready for something! I wish so I could help him, but it's beyond me, far beyond me!" Mamma Young sighed deeply. It was plain she was speaking at last from much pondering in her heart. She came back to the comfort of talking about her boys when they were babies.

"Ralph, now. I honestly felt sorry for the child when I had Harvey while he was such a baby. I re-

member when Harvey came. Gran'ma said: 'No
need for your nose to be outa joint, Son. You be my
boy now.' And she really took almost all the care of
him. When he was little he'd go to her sooner'n he'd
go to me, she took so much care of him. And he's
never forgot it. Ralph's awfully fond of his grandmother. He never loses his patience with her, never.

"I'm glad yours is six years apart and didn't over-
lap so. Betty's gone with her dad and the boys to
watch them put up hay. You don't care, do you? I
said to Tom—jokin', you know—I got him by himself and I said to Tom: 'I'm makin' cherry cobbler,
and if Ralph's young'n comes cryin' from your boys
pickin' on her, not a bite do you get, and I mean it!' "

"I'm going down," Phyllis said, "and stay down
all day, doctor or no doctor. I think Edna's laid up
all these lazy days against me, and it will take all
summer, no matter how hard I try, to make up for
them. I think I'll walk out to where they're haying
after I've bathed the baby."

"Well, that would do you good, likely," Mamma
Young agreed. "The boys got the cherries all picked
now and Edna'n' I are going to pit them soon as we
can get at it. But let me bathe the boy. I'd like to. I
want to weigh him. You go right on out to the field
if you think it's not too long a way. It's so nice out.

Just day after day like this! I can hardly believe it. I feel like they say old Mrs. Morgan does—that we've been forgiven or something. I wake up and it's just a surprise to me to see it so green, after a whole year of it so dead gray. Seems like a miracle. Greenest June I ever saw. Let me take the baby on down—you're not to carry him."

Mamma Young gathered the boy to her soft bosom and went slowly downstairs with him, clucking to him all the way.

Left alone, Phyllis dressed slowly, carefully, in her pink gingham. It was so nice to be putting on her "thin" dresses again. To tie the sash of pink gingham round her very slender waist seemed almost as great a miracle to her as the greenness of the land was to Mamma Young. Ralph might not say anything, he might not even notice enough to *know* he noticed the pink gingham, but he would smile, without bothering to figure out how she was like her old self.

Phyllis had learned in the eight years of her marriage to rejoice in Ralph's noticings and in his splashes of wit when they came, and not to bait him for them. She had not quite learned, however, to let her own happiness in the things she made for their home be enough for her. She still felt angry, ter-

ribly angry, and hurt when Ralph failed to notice
work that had cost her hours of effort and tiredness;
but she was learning. Always after she had been
furious with him for not noticing, not appreciating,
she forgave him and made a last great effort to do
something else, something specially for him, and
found a deep and very superior satisfaction in her
silent forgiveness. Sometimes he gave the needed
irony to that satisfaction by saying, stretched long
and shoeless in the easy chair she had sawed and built
and cushioned for him: "My, Baby, we've got it
mighty cozy here, haven't we?"

The winter was really over and gone. Phyllis
could almost forget it, the brittle cold, the dust, and
the dead ugliness that lay on the land, and the work-
ings of hate in the house. Her boy's coming had
been so much worse than her girl's coming. It was
better not to think of it at all. "A fine boy!" the doctor had said foolishly, like a doctor in a woman's-
magazine story, and when she had laughed with the
mingled mirth at his saying just that and pleasure at
having a fine boy, Ralph had sobbed aloud because
she was still alive and *could* laugh, and somewhere,
away and away, she had heard her father-in-law
shouting to his old mother: "And it's going to rain,
Ma, it's going to rain!" Her fine boy had come the

morning of the day it rained.

When she was dressed she put her room in order. The overalls Ralph had worn the day before lay over the back of the little rocker, chaff spilling from the turned-up cuff. What had he said about their needing mending? They looked like such tired clothes, tired with such a farmer-tiredness. Something about them made her remember the early days of her marriage—those days and those nights when she was getting used to the tiredness of farmers. She wondered if all town girls who married farmers puzzled over it. It was an honest, shoes-off and silent tiredness—that young farmers seemed to be able to lay aside almost entirely through the evenings of their courting days. She had been surprised, but she got used to it and felt at home with it. She had learned to read her poetry books to herself, to fall asleep over her own sewing at nine o'clock.

Edna was alone in the kitchen when Phyllis came down. She grunted something that might have been "Good morning" and went out the kitchen door with a nest of pans under her arm. "Cherries," she said over her shoulder, and Phyllis knew that she meant that the pans were to be used in sorting and pitting the cherries, and that Edna was in one of her kindlier moods.

150

Cleo came out of old Grandma's room with her hair standing out wildly around her pointed face. "Well, you up?" she said when she saw Phyllis. "Thought the doctor said you were to go back to bed and stay there all this week too."

"I feel fine," Phyllis said, "just fine."

Cleo washed at the sink and sat down at the kitchen table with Phyllis and held her cup for Phyllis to pour her some coffee. "You're lucky," she said, "if you feel fine. I sure don't. Couldn't sleep. With the whole yard out there, what did they do but bring all that cherry stuff right round under my window. Mamma and old Gran'ma and Edna out there. They got the baby out there too, on a quilt. Mamma's going on to the baby, and old Gran'ma's talking about her folks in Indiana, and *nobody* could sleep."

"I'm going out and help," Phyllis said; "I love cherry time."

"Well, you can sure have mine," Cleo said. "They likely won't let you help, anyway. Old Gran'ma'll start in about some woman that had a baby and then pitted cherries and the baby died of double convulsions."

Phyllis laughed. "I never heard of those," she said, "but it sounds like her all right."

"Mamma'll likely run in to get a cushion for you."

"*You* should have a baby," Phyllis said, still laughing.

"Me? Like heck I should! Nobody'd be madder'n Harve if I did have one, nobody but me. He's ga-ga about kids—yours anyway—but he wouldn't want me to have one." She slid her chair closer to Phyllis's, rested her elbow on the table and her chin in her palm, and said: "Harve's up to something. I don't know—but he's up to something. He means to put something over on me—you wait, you wait and see. I'm on to him. You wait. Two can play at his game."

"What game?" Phyllis asked.

"You wait," Cleo said, narrowing her usually extra-wide eyes to slits. Cleo always talked to Phyllis when they were alone as though they were allied against the Young forces. She was always saying: "You wait, you just wait." Now she felt in her pockets for cigarettes, and finding none, poured herself another cup of coffee and brooded over it, her shoulders rounded, her mouth pouting.

"Some day that guy's going to get me mad enough I'll tell him a few things," she said. "He needn't think I'll stand this, and stick around here forever. I've had more than one good job and I can get another. I'd get something lined up, and pretty quick, if I got out of here, and don't think I wouldn't."

She picked up a piece of cold toast and bit into it with her narrow teeth. "I was nuts about Harve," she said with sudden plaintiveness, "and he was about me too. He liked my bunch, and he liked me and everything I did, till he started running round with that country-club bunch and met up with that front-page deb. Well, *she* let him down, and I took him back. Not every girl'd do that. He don't know what he wants, Harve Young don't! You don't know Harve from what he's like now. Last summer it was nothing but golf, and now it's reading a book. At first he liked everything I did, and honest, Phyllis, when we got married, before we got out of the courthouse he began to crab, and he's done nothing but beef, and bawl me out, ever since. He thinks he's so smart, and it's the God's truth that guy can't even spell. I had to work his letters over all the time, in the office. I don't kid myself, Harve's about as spoiled and stuck up as a man can get. And what's he got to be so stuck up about? He got spoiled playing football down at the State, and you know all his folks spoil him here. He thinks his family's so much better'n mine, though he's never seen mine. And except for you and Ralph, who round here's so darned educated? Ralph, he had just the two years, didn't he? That's all right, but he don't need to get so superior, Harve don't. Good night, I went to business college, didn't I? I didn't go clear through, but I stepped into a good job that'd turned down graduates."

Phyllis had been waiting for Cleo to finish, listening with vexed pity. "I'm going outside," she said, when she had washed and put away her plate and cup. "I want to help with the cherries."

"You for it," Cleo said. She looked at Phyllis with mingled suspicion and pleading in her face, like a tattling child. "All right," she said, and got up and smoothed her uncombed hair back from her face, "all right, but you wait, just wait and see." She went toward old Grandma's room, leaving her breakfast dishes for Edna to wash.

Out in the sunshine the three women, Mamma Young, old Grandma Young, and Edna, made a bright picture grouped round the baskets and pans of cherries. Mamma Young was in faded green gingham, Edna in blue percale, and old Grandma in her black sateen, white apron, and Paisley shawl. Mamma Young sometimes tried to get old Grandma to fold her Paisley shawl away, declaring that it was far too good for every day, but old Grandma always

said: "No, I learned my lesson looking into old Mrs. Tickert's casket. Look how she skimped and saved and was just a living patch, and when they buried her, did she have her good shawl on? No, she didn't. Those boys' wives of hers, they thought it was too good. And if they'd buried her in it, what comfort would it've been? No, I tell you, my Aunt Kate was right: 'Have the best first and have the best all the time.' I'll wear my good shawl. I don't go out often, and when I do I'll wear it and get the good of it. It'll outlast me," she would say. "It's a good piece of cashmere."

Phyllis dropped down on the folded quilt beside her baby and reached for a handful of cherries.

"That's right," Mamma Young said, "eat all you want. They'll never harm you. Some say they will, but they won't, not if you don't drink milk the same meal they won't. I remember one of the Miller girls —they're all gone now—had the prettiest color, and they say that's what she did in cherry time. Drank a quart of cherry juice every day. They used to put it up, they say, put the cherries through the press and put up the juice, just for her to have to drink. My, she was a pretty girl! You remember her, don't you, Gran'ma?"

" 'Deed I do," old Grandma said, sucking loudly

on a cherry, "and she was lazy as sin. All those Miller girls was lazy and she was the worst. I remember we had one of them over once, and the river came up and she couldn't get home for a week, and instead of helpin' me, I had to pick up after her. She'd stand and look in the mirror, primpin', with the men right in the room. Edith, her name was."

"Oh, no, Gran'ma," Mamma Young said. "That wasn't Edith. Edith was one of the older ones, and goodness knows she wasn't lazy or silly about her looks either. That was Grace was the one that was at your house."

"You don't know a thing about it," old Grandma said sharply, and drew her shawl closer about her elbows. "That was before you were born. This girl, this Grace, was a little thing, something like this woman George brought home, only dark instead of fair, and she was lazy as sin."

Mamma Young began to hum a hymn. It was scarcely worth her while on such a fair morning to take the time to remind her mother-in-law that she was not her "born" child, that Cleo was Harvey's wife, not long-lost George's, and that she herself had just owned that the Miller girl they had been discussing was Grace and not Edith.

"The best ones," Edna explained, "go in this pan,

for pickles. The pitted ones, here."

Phyllis felt reproved for eating instead of pitting, and after she had kissed her baby's wrist, straightened up and began to work rapidly. "I'm glad there'll be so much for pickles," she said. "I think your cherry pickles are the best I ever ate."

"They are good," Mamma Young said, "but they're not mine; that is, the receipt isn't. No, those are Jenny's mother's pickles, and she made up the receipt herself."

"Jenny?" Phyllis said. "Now, she's a cousin, isn't she?" Phyllis had much enjoyed getting acquainted with the Young relatives through hearsay.

"Well, yes," Mamma Young said, "she's a cousin in a way, for she's married to one of Arch's brother Jim's boys, but she's no blood relation. But Jenny's mother—her name was Jenny too—she was dearer to me than I could think a sister would be, though I never had a sister. They came out here about the third year Arch and I were married, I think, shortly after Gran'ma moved in with us, and we just took to each other from the start, Jenny and I. Oh, she was the best woman!"

"Who you talkin' about?" old Grandma asked, hitching her chair closer to Mamma Young's. "You mean Jenny Blight? Well, I don't know how you

158

can say it, Mamie. I never liked her. I never could abide a woman that wouldn't stay home and tend to her own house, and that woman was over here a good half of the time."

"Oh, no, she wasn't, Gran'ma," Mamma Young said. She shook the pan on her lap, to settle the pitted cherries, and then held the pan out to Edna and dropped her hands either side of her, with the juice dripping from her fingers, and said to Phyllis: "Sometimes I'd give anything to see that old white mare and that buggy come over the hill, up there by the cottonwood. I miss Jenny so."

"I never think of her," old Grandma said with decision, and put her hands behind her to grasp the back of the rocker to help herself up. "I'm going in," she said. "I'm going in and lie down awhile."

Edna went with Grandma. "Time to get the potatoes peeled," she said.

Alone with her mother-in-law and her baby, Phyllis stretched out on the quilt and lay with her hands clasped under her head.

"Gran'ma's never got over it," Mamma Young said, and laughed silently, quiveringly. "She never liked Jenny—that's Jenny's mother I'm speaking of now. You see, I wasn't but seventeen when Arch and I were married, and we lived in a little frame

159

house that they tore down when they built-over the cow barn, and then when Jim got married— that's a funny thing for Jim—he named his boy after himself, his first boy, and Jenny, this friend of mine, she named her girl after herself, and they grew up and were married. We used to call them Big Jenny and Little Jenny, but Jenny wasn't a big woman; she was little. Little Jenny's a lot like her, but she'd never have the get-up and go that Jenny had. You see, we were planning the house, this house here, and Gran'ma, her mind was all made up, and she'd tell Arch just how she wanted things built. I was just a girl, and I wasn't asked 'Ay, yes or no?' Arch—you know how he is yet. He thinks everything's smooth, and Gran'ma'd run him. She run all her boys. He never dreamed but I was per- fectly satisfied. And, Phyllis, I couldn't even wring out a dish-rag but Gran'ma would take it outa my hand and tell me how they wrung their dish-rags in Indiana!

"Well, Jenny came out here with Mr. Blight, and she was from Connecticut, and first time she was over here, Gran'ma started in on Indiana, and Jenny started in on Connecticut, and it was just a show, and so noticeable even Arch noticed. We got out the plans we'd drawn up for the house, or that

Gran'ma'd drawn up, rather, with Arch saying: 'Well, just whatever you and Mamie want, Ma,' and Jenny could see I'd not had a word, and she lit in, sayin': 'How'd *you* want this, Mamie?' and I thought Gran'ma was going to put 'em out. I had to ask 'em to stay for supper myself. She wouldn't.

"Why, I was such a goose, wanting so much to please Arch. And if Jenny'd never come out here, she'd be runnin' me yet, Gran'ma would. Jenny showed me the way. 'Sing a hymn,' she said to me, 'and go your own way, Mamie,' and I've done it. Jenny was a great one to be fixing around her house. If she wanted anything, she took the odds and ends on hand and she made it. You put me in mind of her, Phyllis, in that. The day you fixed over the ell room for you and Ralph and Betty, I said to Arch: 'Now, that's Jenny for you, all over!' I know you can't tell a young girl just starting up housekeeping anything, but if you could, I think that's what I'd tell her—what Jenny told me: 'Sing a hymn, and go your own way.' A man's good for some things, but for knowing what a woman's about when she's making something—well, you know. What comfort are they? There ain't one in a hundred'll come and say: 'Ain't that nice—and what a lot of work!' Not unless he's been prompted a lot or is a kind of old granny anyway. No, it's a neighbor you got to look to for that. There's nothing like a good neighbor. And there never was one fuller of appreciation than Jenny was.

"Her girl's been on my mind a lot lately, since those floods started out west. Jim and Little Jenny live out near McCook, you know, out there where it's bad. I knew when Arch subscribed to the paper again, after we'd done without it for so long, that there was something he just had to know about, and it's those floods, and his brother's boy out there in 'em. But their names haven't been listed, and I guess if they'd been washed out and were alive they'd let us know. I guess they must be all right."

"Have they never been back here?" Phyllis asked.

"Oh, yes, they've been here a number of times, before and since my Jenny died, on their way to the Fair. Jenny's got two of the huskiest little girls." Here Mamma Young stopped to laugh, her silent, bosom-shaking laugh. "I wish you could have seen," she said. "Jenny's oldest girl's just the age of Edna's first boy, you know. Well, when they were here last—Tom and Edna were still in their own house then—we had them all over here for supper. The children went out to play and

Tommy tried to take something Jenny's girl had, and he come in yelling so and dripping blood all over the kitchen. She'd taken him down and trounced him good—bloodied his nose. They're sturdy little things, and they're a little like their grandma. They know their own mind."

"I was going to the hayfield," Phyllis said. "Do you think it's too near dinner time?"

"Why, I don't know," Mamma Young said. "I'd guess it isn't more'n eleven. Better feed your boy first, and then, if you don't think it's too warm, you go. Wear my hat."

Phyllis took the baby into the house to nurse him. Edna was setting the table. Old Grandma was sleeping on her bed in the kitchen corner, snoring her trembling, feeble snores. Awake, she seemed very much alive, but always when she slept Phyllis was reminded of the old woman's age and fragility. There were pauses between snores that seemed alarmingly long at times.

"Guess they'll think they got the whole family out there," Edna said, when Phyllis told her she was going to the hayfield. "Your girl and my kids out there now. The boys are helping, of course."

The anger Edna's words could bring rose in Phyllis. Did Edna think Betty had no business out at the hayfield even when her father took her there —that the child would be in the way? The baby squirmed in her arms. In the corner old Grandma turned on her back and snored a louder, whistling snore. Phyllis was reminded of the old woman's warning that anger would "bitter" her milk.

When Phyllis started toward the stair door with her baby, Edna said: "Where you goin'? You wait. I'll carry the basket down. You'd rather have him downstairs, wouldn't you?"

Kindness from Edna always touched Phyllis. Kindness came so hard to Edna. "Why don't you go out with me," Phyllis asked, "out to the hayfield?"

"Me!" Edna said. "Say, I haven't been out there since the year I was married." She laughed her breathy laugh. "Used to work in the field all the time 'fore I was married. Would yet, only Tom's mother's got notions about it. Thinks it looks funny! Anyway, somebody's got to get the dinner. No—I'll stay here."

When she had put the baby in his basket, Phyllis took her mother-in-law's wide straw hat and went out and through the barnyard to the hayroad. She stopped by the garden fence to look at the rows of peas and beans, the lettuce, and the melon plants.

The garden was clear of weeds and fine-looking. Phyllis swung her hat from her fingertips and wondered who it was that kept the garden. Edna, she supposed. Yes, she was sure that many times when the little boys had asked for their mother, Mamma Young had said: "Why, she's up at the garden, I believe." Edna carried the burden of the housework, did the washings and ironings, looked after her chickens, and managed, without talking about it, to keep a garden.

The hayroad left its years-old ruts to curve round a stagnant, muddy pool. A black-and-white cow came to the fence and stretched out her neck and breathed loudly toward Phyllis. Her childhood horror of cows came on her so that she wanted to run. "Sook Boss, Sook Boss!" she said, put out her hand, then drew it back from the wet, slobbery tongue, and was glad no Young, even Ralph, was near to see her.

Seeing Edna's garden, and now her fear of the cow, brought over Phyllis a not unfamiliar loneliness and humility. She was not one of the Youngs. Not in her life would she grow to be one of them. She remembered a night of troubling and heartsearching during the time of her engagement. Ralph had read aloud to her a letter from his mother about cooking for threshers, canning, and sewing, and she had realized what her life was likely to be and how unready she was for it. She had lain awake the night, and the next evening, after a bad day at school, she had tried to give Ralph back his ring, tried to tell him, in honesty and fear, that she was not a fit wife for him, that she had not the hardihood to work as his mother worked, and had only skill for making things nice, and that she did not want to spoil his life. But she had wept in the telling, at the awfulness of giving him up, and he had taken her in his arms and told her she was "a goose" and "all tired out." It had changed nothing. The next morning on her way to school how the meadow larks had sung in the fields! Two of her first-grade pupils had waited at the corner for her, two sturdy, pink-faced little sisters with tow braids. One was named Ann; she had put her hand on Ann's warm smooth hair and had felt happy in the thought of her coming marriage. She would have children like Ann, she would make everything nice in her house, and surely grace and strength would be given her.

The hayfield was beyond the "near" wheatfield. There was a gentle, cool wind on the fields that made ripples over the grain. Beyond the wheat she saw the stacks on the alfalfa-field, and the slowly rising stacker. She heard the men shouting to their horses. Ralph's loud: "Get over there, Kit, you!" surprised her, amused her just as it always did. Not in the eight years of her marriage had he ever been "cross" with her, ever raised his voice in anger. She always started a little when he yelled at the stock.

The wheat came up to her breast. She felt suddenly free of it, as though she had been wanting to run, when the hayroad led into the open alfalfa-field.

Harvey saw her first—he was on the stack—and waved to her. Ralph was driving his sweep, an extra large load of hay before his team. She stopped near the stack and watched him come on. Kit and Beaut stopped just where they should, then backed expertly, and the stacker rose slowly and slid its burden of hay onto the stack. The timbers of the buck were red, and its teeth bone-white against the very blue sky. There was something fine about the stacker's going up, emptying, and then going slowly down.

Little Betty came running to her mother, rubbed her hot cheek against Phyllis's wrist, and cried: "Mother, I didn't know *you* were coming. Look! Look what Daddy found! A pheasant egg! She had a nest and they spoiled it, but they didn't mean to. Daddy says she'll make another one. The other eggs are in Tommy's hat."

"No, they ain't," Tommy said, puffing from running to get to Phyllis before his brothers could reach her; "we threw 'em."

"Oh, *no!*" cried Betty.

"Sure we did," Tommy gloated. "Busted 'em. Threw 'em at a post."

Betty began to cry. "I was going to take 'em home," she sobbed. "I was going to put 'em under a hen."

"We'll put this one under," Phyllis said. "Don't cry. Shall I hold it for you? You've held it, kept it warm, haven't you?"

Betty ran away to look for other pheasant nests that she confided to her mother she'd likely "never, never" find, and the boys went to follow their father's mower. Phyllis sat down on a heap of cut alfalfa and rested, her arms wound about her knees. Watching, it was easy for her to understand how Edna had been happy, helping in the haying. The thought of doing the work herself tired her, but to imagine Edna doing it, stacking, up on the stack, or driving the sweep, filled her with a vicarious happiness.

168

Ralph came to her at once when the men stopped work. "My, you look slick as a banana peel, Baby," he said, giving the lie to her pre-breakfast thoughts about his reactions to the pink dress and her regained slimness. He dropped into the stubble beside her. "How do you feel?" he asked. "This the day Doc said you could be up?"

"Your mother said I could," Phyllis said. "I feel fine."

Harvey came over to them, his face grimy from the dust of the hay. "Hello!" he grinned. "You don't look like a farm girl. Tell you what you look like— like the lead in a bucolic operetta." He drew down his mouth, wrinkling his brows, and said in his brother Tom's serious, vexed voice: "Come *on*, let's get going!"

"You can ride in the cart," Ralph said, pointing toward the decrepit rig that pulled the buck. "You and Betty."

"No, no she's not to," Harvey said. "She's to ride old Tilly. And I'll ride Prince. Come on."

"Why, I could never get up on her," Phyllis said, more than half afraid. "I—"

Tom had driven his team near. At his grave "Hello, Phyllis. Come on, boys, let's get going," Harvey laughed, picked Phyllis up, and swung her onto old Tilly's back. "I'll take this team," he said to Tom, and got on Prince.

"You'll look after Betty?" Phyllis called back to Ralph, not at all sure he was pleased at his brother's highhandedness. Ralph grinned after them, a grin that was an answer to Harvey's. Harvey was the favored one. Whatever he did was in the eyes of Ralph and Tom and Grandpa Young right enough and endearing.

"I abducted you like this so I could talk to you," Harvey said. "Got something to tell you."

Phyllis remembered her talk with Cleo that morning and waited, clinging to the harness, which made a very insecure side-saddle, and anxious about riding. It would make her unforgivably ridiculous to fall off a work-horse, at a "dead walk."

"I think I'm getting out," Harvey said. "I oughta know any day. I think I got a job!" His voice grew husky with the import of his news, with the hope of having a job. "And I got to go alone if I go," he said. In his embarrassment he gave old Prince a crack with the rein, and both horses trotted a few paces. Phyllis grasped the harness more tightly and did not try to speak until the horses were walking again.

"Oh—fine!" she gasped. "Fine! Tell me about it!"

"Well, a fellow I was in school with wrote me.

Says he's got a job down in New Mexico, a good one, a soil-erosion job, and in the place where he is they need an accountant, and he put my name in, wrote me, and I got the application blank and filled it out and sent it in, and—he thinks I got a good chance of getting it. If I do—I go down there—and the men live in barracks."

"What—what about Cleo?" Phyllis asked.

"Well, I'll send her money, but I can't take her down there. There's no place for her." Harvey was looking, not at Phyllis, but away over the fields, with such satisfaction in his face that Phyllis could not help feeling some pity for Cleo.

"I thought you and Cleo were getting on a lot better, that you were happier," she said.

"You mean, by any chance, that look she gets in her eye when I do something she's thought up to see if she can make me do?" Harvey asked. "Nope, after that night Dad bawled us out, I made up my mind—two things: first, I was getting *out*, just as soon as I could, and second, I wasn't going to give the folks any more of Cleo's shows than I could help."

"I think she's very lonesome," Phyllis said, surprised at herself, little as she found to like about Cleo, to be seeming to champion her.

"Who isn't?" Harvey asked. "It's her own doing.

I'd have got on with her if she'd tried at all, but she hasn't. I'm like Dad. I don't like scrapping. The only way for Cleo to be happy is to be on the go all the time and be scrapping in between. We haven't the time or the money for that. Aw, Phyllis, you know there's no sense in me tryin' to get on with a girl like Cleo! I've tried it a whole winter—and that's too long. I thought if I couldn't have Doris it didn't make much difference who I had. But that, even, wouldn't have been what I wanted. I couldn't ever *talk* to Doris. She'd make you feel all the time that things were all right for right now, but you'd better look out, in a minute you'd likely do something to make her walk off and never come back. I guess she was just spoiled." He smiled suddenly, that broad smile that all the Youngs found irresistible. "And her golf was rotten," he said, "and I couldn't tell her a thing. No, I'm going to get loose, and then I'm going to look for a girl like you, Phyllis."

She turned and looked at him again, her lips parted, her eyes wide with surprise at the earnestness in his voice.

"Don't you do it, Harvey," she said, her words tumbling over one another. "I'm spoiled too, rotten spoiled, as old Gran'ma says. I'm an awful baby. I can't garden and I'm scared of cows, scared sick!"

Harvey looked down at her, and they laughed together, loudly, happily. There was the rattle of cartwheels behind them, and Ralph and little Betty turned out round them, into the edge of the field. Tom and his boys came up behind them too. Then there was the garden and beyond that the barnyard, and next Ralph was putting up his arms and saying: "I'm afraid you're doing too much, Baby. You ought to take it easy."

The spicy smell of pickle syrup drowned out the odor of fried potatoes and ham. Ralph went to admire his young son, where he lay in his basket at the foot of old Grandma's bed, and Grandpa picked up his paper, even before he looked over his few pieces of mail, to see what there was about the floods.

There was a letter by Harvey's plate. The boy picked it up and went out onto the step with·it and did not come in even when Tom called him. Grandpa asked the blessing without either Harvey or Cleo at the table, and then opened his letters with his table-knife. "Letter from Jim here, Mamma," he said to Mamma Young. "Let's see what he says."

"Well, I'm glad," Mamma Young said, "awful glad. I've had Jenny on my mind and heart so all this week, especially this morning. Does seem, if there *was* anything—"

"Well, well, Mamma, listen to this," Grandpa said, "listen to this, Mamma—they been clear washed out!" Instead of reading the letter aloud, he handed it over to his wife.

"Jim has?" old Grandma cried. She was always confusing her *son* Jim with her grandson Jim. "Well, I told him not to go out there. The Republican's a tricky river. Any river's tricky, and the farther off one I live, the better I like it; but I'm sorry for Jim, I am. But Jim's gone, isn't he? I thought we buried Jim, Arch. Didn't we lay Jim away?" She was almost crying, lost between reality and things she "musta dreamed."

Harvey came in from the steps. At just that minute, as though she had heard him walking about and thought he would be coming for her, Cleo came from old Grandma's room.

Harvey went to his place, slid a generous slice of ham onto his plate, and then sat looking at them, his large hands resting, tremblingly, either side his plate. "Dad," he said, "I got a job."

"Oh, dear," Mamma Young said, with such a mingling of meaning. She was happy, of course, that Harvey had a job, but a job would take their baby away from them, and they had loved having him home, even for such a bad and crowded winter, even with Cleo.

"Ya?" Cleo said through her pointed teeth. "What?"

"Well, that's good, Son," Grandpa Young said, "but we'll be sorry to have you go if you have to leave." Grandpa Young spoke with ease and love and hospitality, as a man who had plenty of money and a big house might speak.

Phyllis, looking at him, saw him through tears and loved him almost as much as she loved her own father.

"What is it?" Cleo shrilled. "What's your job?"

Harvey looked at her. Was the moment of his telling his family about his job to be spoiled by a woman who had somehow come to plague his days, a woman who screeched at him?

He half rose in his chair. "Will you shut up?" he said. "Will you shut your mouth just a minute?"

Mamma Young gasped. It was the first time since the night Phyllis's boy was born, the night Grandpa had told the boys "where to head in," the night before it had rained, that Harvey had told Cleo to shut up.

"What's the matter with you?" Tom asked. "She

didn't do anything. She just asked you what you're going to do. What's wrong with that? Whata you have to take her head off for?"

The letter, Harvey's letter, lay beside his plate. He had taken it from his pocket and put it there while Tom was talking to him.

"Now you keep out of this," he said with forced calmness. "Cleo's my wife, not yours. I'll be glad to tell her what I'm going to do if she'll keep still and let me." His voice was not only angry, but hurt. He was the baby, and what he did was important and interesting in the eyes of his family. He had wanted a job so long, and now a near miracle, a pure happenstance, had brought him one, and his wife and his brother were spoiling it for him.

Mamma Young gave a bosomy mother-moan, and held Nephew Jim's letter up in her hands. She had looked down at the letter in her embarrassment when Harvey and Tom were quarreling, and the line she saw was: "And all Jenny's mother's things gone, dishes and all."

"Listen, children!" she said. "Jim and Jenny's homeless, clear homeless!" She looked round at them, her tears running over. "What'll we do, Arch, we'll have to send for 'em, won't we?"

"Where d'you think you'd put 'em?" Edna asked. "Looks to me—"

"They can have Gran'ma's room," Harvey said. "I'm packin' right now."

"Oh, Son, I'll have to do some mending for you," Mamma Young said, "and I think you'll just have to buy you some socks. Yours are riddled."

Harvey handed his letter, the letter that gave him a job and his hope of freedom, across to his father, and his eyes asked forgiveness for losing his temper at the table. The old man adjusted his glasses, coughed and whistled, and then read slowly.

Phyllis's baby cried, and she went to him. In the excitement about the two letters no one noticed when she lifted him and carried him upstairs herself. She put him in the middle of the big bed and lay down beside him.

"Happy birthday, happy birthday!" she said to him. "Did everybody but his mamma forget it was his birthday?" He looked up at the rafters with solemn, blue eyes wide. His gaze was like her father's, for all his brief four weeks. She lay brushing his wisp of hair with a finger until his eyes closed and he was asleep again.

She was glad she had not stayed for the reading

177

aloud of Jenny's and Jim's letters. She did not feel strong enough in heart or body for listening to letters about floods and losses, no matter how courageous the letters might be. She knew just how they would begin: "Dear Uncle Arch, Aunt Mamie, and all—" Mamma Young had a slow, come-what-may monotone for letters from dear ones read aloud. Phyllis had particularly wanted a letter from her father, and none had come. Any letter from him would be very like the last, brief and much like a business letter. Only one who loved him could know the despair the time-worn phrases covered. She felt a pity for him as helpless as that Mamma Young felt for Harvey, and more hopeless. She saw his long white fingers rolling his watch-chain, and his lean chin set. He had been a man men trusted and turned to, and now his active life was over. All letters that came to the Young house, whether of a social or business nature, were of family interest and were usually read aloud at the dinner-table and enjoyed and discussed, all but Phyllis's and Cleo's. Phyllis had shared her friends' letters with the family, but not her father's. The Youngs' misfortunes were to be lived through and the burden of them shared, with the hope that everything would be better by and by, possibly soon. Her father's defeat carried no such hope, and her sorrow in it was a sacred one, too keen and proud for sharing.

In the tipped dresser mirror she could see herself, very slender in her pink dress. She might be some young girl, holding somebody else's baby. She put her hand to her face and brushed back the curls. It seemed to her that she had not looked so young since the spring Ralph had given her his ring. There was a sleepy, noonday mingling of birds in the yard trees. Overhead, against the rafters, a wasp buzzed and blundered. How good it was that spring, and as much of the summer as they had, had been so pleasantly cool! Only two nights had the raftered room been too hot for sleeping. Ralph had slept even then.

Now she heard Ralph coming up to her. His feet sounded lighter on the stair. Maybe it was Harvey instead of Ralph, coming up to tell her about his new job. Wasn't she a goose, though, to be so flattered that Harvey thought he wanted a girl like her when he picked another? Poor boy, she was sorry for him, sorry for Cleo too, sorry for the Jim Youngs, who were washed out, sorry to tears. She wiped the tears away with the hem of her baby's dress and smiled up at Ralph when he came in.

He sat down on the bed beside her.

"Well," he said, looking at the sleeping baby,

"Whata you think of that stack? Pretty nice stack, wasn't it?"

"Fine," Phyllis said, looking at him through wet lashes.

He glanced about the room. "You know, I think we could cut a couple of dormer windows in here," he said. "If they've got to sleep up here they'll roast if we don't get some more windows in."

"Who?" Phyllis asked. "Who's going to sleep up here?"

"Why, Jim and Jenny, and their girls, I guess."

"Well, I guess not! Where are *we* going to sleep? If you think I'll move back down to old Gran'ma's room—Ralph, I won't. I—"

Ralph leaned over and brought his face close to hers. There was a strong smell of alfalfa, sweat, and horses about him. "Will you shut your mouth?" he growled, in a voice that was much like Harvey's voice for Cleo, and laid his cheek against hers. "If you weren't such a little pig, I'd have had a surprise for you," he said, "and now I suppose I'll have to tell you."

"Ralph," she whispered, "you're not going—*you* haven't got a job down there too?"

"Nope. Don't want one. But we got a house." He

sat up again to look at her, to see what she thought about their having a house.

"Where?" she breathed.

"Over other side of Don Ferguson's. It's two rooms, Baby. Their renter-house, and they're not going to have renters any more. I'm fetchin' it over just as soon as we get through haying. See?"

"Oh, my!" Phyllis said happily, ready to cry again. "Ralph, you're—how are you going to pay for it?"

"With the sweat of my brow, and Dad's and Tom's. Harvey gets off, since he's leaving tonight. We're going to work it out over there. It's just two rooms. You mustn't expect much."

"I'll love it," Phyllis said. "Has it any closets?"

"I never noticed, Baby. It's got two rooms, and the paper's all off, or hanging."

He leaned and kissed her, and Phyllis, busy with the happiness of feeling so well and slim, so proud of her baby, so in love with Ralph, had mind enough left, with her arms tight about Ralph's neck, to remember the bundle of wallpaper in the storeroom behind the quilt curtains. There must be two dozen rolls. Would there be rolls enough alike to paper one of the rooms? Most likely not. But even with three rolls alike she could panel the rooms. She could distribute the other patterns, the gayer patterns, in panels. She could . . .

Tom was calling Ralph at the stair door. He kissed her again and looked at her with that awed, enraptured look, as he had looked at her the morning her son was born, as though God had held her back from another world for him. She got to her feet and went to the door with him and hugged him as hard as she could before she let him go.

As soon as the lower stair door closed on him, she went into the storeroom and found the bundle of wallpaper and untied the binding twine that held it. There her mother-in-law found her, with the wallpaper in scrolls around her.

"Oh, dear, oh, dear!" the old lady said, sat down on a trunk, and smoothed her apron over her knees with her plump hands. "I've got so much to do I don't know where to begin. I got to mend Harvey's shirts and underclothes, and the boy's plain destitute of socks. He's going on the night train too. This friend of his sent him a check. Wasn't that mighty fine?"

"And what about Cleo?"

"Oh," Mamma Young looked down at the wallpaper patterns as though she'd quite forgotten Cleo.

182

"You know how old that piece is?" she asked. "Arch got that paper and we papered our bedrooms with it the spring we lost the baby. Didn't say a word, just brought the paper home. Awfully pretty, isn't it? And it did comfort me, somehow it did."

Phyllis waited.

"Why, she acted up," Mamma Young said, "Cleo did, awful. She got excited and said to Harve: 'You'll see, you'll see! You'll not leave me stuck off out here. I'll get out too!' Talked like Harvey was leaving her or something. She said she'd not stand it, not stay on, that he wasn't the only one had plans. I think she held it against him he wrote and found out about that job without telling her what he was up to. And you can't blame him for that. A job's such an uncertain thing. Why, he hadn't even told his pa or me. She was so bitter to him, such talk and carrying on!"

"She loves him," Phyllis said, imagining and then rejecting as too horrible for thought Ralph's planning to go away from her and then being so obviously relieved and happy in the going.

"That may be. Yes, I guess she does," Mamma Young said. "But she's got a queer way of showing it, Phyllis. Harve's gentle like Arch, really, and if she'd ever've put herself out, really, to be nice and make it comfortable and pleasant for him— You wonder how anybody ever brought a girl up to act so. And I'm sorry for her, but I'm glad too, for Tom's sake. You know how Tom's been. He's tender-hearted, for all he's so short-spoken sometimes, and feels for anybody that's helpless. People can work on his sympathy. They can, you know, and I think he's never really *seen* Cleo, clear. And when she lit into Harve like she did, well, Tom just *looked* at her. He got up and walked out of the house. Maybe I imagined it, but it seemed to me it had kinda opened his eyes. I don't think he'll let his sympathies run away from him so again."

Mamma Young smoothed her dress under her pink fingers while she talked. Not for her life would she have owned, even to Phyllis, that one of her sons had been more than half in love with another son's wife, but she had to express her relief that the anxiety she had felt was over, for the time at least.

"What will she *do*?" Phyllis asked.

"I don't know. He's in her room, getting ready for me to help him pack, and she's in there too, talking to him, crying too, sounds like. Poor boy! She's all unstrung. It's hard on him. He's not got enough to give her money to go away, anywhere, and he knows it's hard for her to stay, and hard for us to have her, after she's shown so clear how she feels about being here. She said she'd get out too, but I think that's all talk. Nobody's more against separation than I am, Phyllis; we've not had it in

the family, in Arch's family or mine; but I don't know . . ."

"Will she stay on in Gran'ma's room?"

"No, no, she won't. There's no sense in it. To-morrow morning I'm going to clean the room and

185

put Gran'ma back in it. Till she goes, if she goes, Cleo can sleep in the kitchen."

A smile was twitching the corners of Mamma Young's mouth. Now Phyllis slid toward the older woman, laid her head back on her knees, and they laughed together, laughed at the thought of Edna coming down to get breakfast in a room where Cleo slept.

"I was talking with the boys," Mamma Young said, "and they think this stuff up here we can store away in the mow, and this end the room we'll use for the little girls, Jenny's little girls. No tellin' how long they'll be with us, but until late fall, I expect."

"And what about *me*?" Phyllis asked.

"You're a bad one!" Mamma Young said. "Don't you think anybody'd know, to look at you, Ralph had told you about that house? Where you going to set it?"

"Oh, up under the cottonwoods, where I went the day before the baby came—that would be nice."

"And haul water all that way? You can't do that, child. It'll have to be nearer the well."

"Down near the apple trees, then."

"That would be all right. We'll see, we'll see. Ralph'll likely have some notions about it, and Arch."

186

"Have you seen it? Has it any closets?" she asked.

"Child, it's bare as a bone," Mamma Young said. "It hasn't a closet or a shelf or anything. It hasn't even a step. I must get downstairs. Edna'll have all the dishes done and set away, and she has enough to do with the cherries on her hands. Betty's asleep in old Gran'ma's bed, with that egg in her fist. I guess she run herself tired this morning."

"I'll come down. I'll come down and help with the cherries," Phyllis said, "as soon as I get this paper rolled up again."

"Arch is writing Jim tonight," Mamma Young said. "They're with some friends of theirs out there."

Phyllis looked up at Mamma Young, shaking her head slowly, wonderingly, at her cheerful acceptance of the idea of having four new people in the house.

"You'll like Jenny," Mamma Young said. "And Jim'll be like one of our own boys. Jenny is such a hand with the canning. And Betty'll like the little girls." She stopped on her way toward the door, to lean over the bed and say: "He's such a good baby. Gran'ma's lamb."

SECOND FALL: PHYLLIS was
sweeping the front room of the little new house, a
great heap of coiled wallpaper scraps before her
broom, when she saw her mother-in-law coming
down the path with a fan of letters in her hand. She
leaned the broom against the window-casing and
went to the door to meet her.

"Did you ever?" Mamma Young panted. "You'd
think there was something to draw people to think
of you, a certain day, to bring so many letters, now
wouldn't you? And this isn't all. There was one for
Cleo, an airmail, special delivery. Now, wouldn't

you think anybody'd know they wouldn't deliver from town clear out here? You know what Cleo did, Phyllis? She got up, for shame, I guess, at the menfolks seeing her still in bed in the kitchen at breakfast time, and went and piled in old Gran'ma's bed. Still sleeping! Betty took the letter in to her. It wasn't from Harvey. She'll take waking up, or anything else, from that child she'd not take from the rest of us. She's really fond of Betty."

Mamma Young sat down in the doorway and spread the letters in her ample lap. "One from my boy!" she said with great satisfaction. "I had a feeling we'd hear from Harvey today. One from Jenny, dear girl. This one for Ralph is from that boy was in school with him he's kept in touch with."

Phyllis stooped and picked up her letter from her father and slid it into her apron pocket, to read when alone again.

"Oh, dear," Mamma Young said, "Harvey's is addressed to his father, and it begins just: 'Dear Papa.'" She reluctantly put the letter back in the envelope. "And likely not a word of it that isn't for us all! Shall I read you Jenny's aloud?"

Phyllis would have liked to wait until noon for the family's enjoyment of Cousin Jenny's letter, but she knew it would give Mamma Young pleasure to read it to her, so she sat down on the step beside her to listen.

"Oh, dear," Mamma Young sighed happily, ready for anything, and began:

"Denver, Colorado, September 17th. Dear Aunt Mamie, Uncle Arch, and all: We were so glad to have your good letters and to know that you are well and that the boys got the renter-place moved for Ralph and Phyllis. I think I remember the house. Out beyond Ferguson's stables, wasn't it? It was like you to write us again to come if we needed. We may have to pull up and come yet. Who knows! It all depends on whether or not Jim's job holds out. They are laying men off every day. If we did have to come, how we'd get the money to make the move, clear from here, I've no notion. I guess I wrote you that when Derrick wrote Jim he thought he could get him on here Jim wanted me to take the girls and come to you until he had something certain, but I just couldn't do it. I found a ride out for us and so the move cost little. The room we have is nothing to talk about, but it is a place to eat and sleep—a roof over us. The girls like their school, now they are getting acquainted. The dresses you sent I got made over for them. I cut them out and sewed them up on a neighbor's machine and then ran her up a couple of house dresses to make it right. Jim feels fine and is standing the work well. It is pretty hard on him to work under a foreman. There's something in Young blood that goes against being told what to do next about work, especially when there is a better way to do it. They have hoed thir *own* rows too many generations, I guess. But he has the job. At least he had it yesterday and went to work this morning. The house next door shuts off the sun and mountains. The Derricks said they would come some Sunday and take the little girls for a drive and I hope they don't forget it. Jim misses the car even more than I do my sewing machine. I suppose they are keeping each other company in the mud somewhere along the Republican. Don't worry about us. Love to you all. Jenny."

Mamma Young slowly folded the letter. "That blue serge of mine, I never wear it, and it is almost as good as new. We must ask her to send the little girls' patterns so we can make them up a dress apiece of it. To think of Jenny without her machine! You can't hardly realize a flood, can you? Seems when the news dies down and the water's gone down it's over, and it's hard to think of the damage *lasting*."

"I know," Phyllis said, her hand on her father's letter.

191

Mamma Young tapped Harvey's letter against her knee. "Harvey's sent a check," she said proudly. "Made out to his father. Forty-five dollars! Now, would you think the boy could spare that much? He must be skimping and figuring like everything."

She stood up and looked into the little house. "I declare, Phyllis," she said, "it looks grand. How you ever got the paper on so smooth, hangin' it all alone, I don't see. Wallpaper Abbie herself couldn't have done better."

"And who is Wallpaper Abbie?" Phyllis asked, ready to take to her heart another of the people Mamma Young had known and liked and made live for her. "Another Young?"

"Young! I should say she wasn't. She was a kind of a gypsy, though too hard-working a woman to be called that. She had an old team and a covered wagon, and what do you think that wagon was covered with? Scene canvas; opera-house curtains! *He'd* been a curtain-painter. Before we knew her she had him to look after too. He wasn't much account, and sick and a burden. When he died she took over his paints and his work, though it was a lot more papering than painting she did. Had a whole raft of children, and all those youngsters would come pilin' out of that wagon and people'd

feed them while Abbie papered." She laughed and wiped the back of her hand across her mouth. "Oh, dear," she went on, "I remember there was a neighbor, she's gone now, had a difference, past speaking, with Arch's mother, and when she found Abbie'd put the same paper on their parlors, she tore hers off with her own hands and shut the room up until Abbie came the next spring. I wonder what ever happened to Abbie, and all those children! First woman I ever saw wear trousers. She was a law unto herself, Abbie was. Aren't you getting awfully tired, Phyllis? You've worked so hard and steady, these three days now?

"I've not let myself think about it yet," Phyllis said. "I seem to have more strength for making something, for fixing something, than I have for anything else. If I worked this hard at plain housework I suppose I'd be ready to drop. I think I'll hold out until it's done and we're moved in."

"Well, I must get on in the house," Mamma Young said, "and help Edna. She's making up the apples the boys brought in into apple butter. Can't you smell it? You could if you were closer to the house. I wish you *had* set the house closer to us. Edna makes a good butter, but I like it a little spicier and sweeter than she makes it.

"You'll have to ask the Fergusons over to take a look when you get moved in and curtains up. They'll never know the place. You've made a real house of it. Are you going to wash the windows and woodwork now? I'll carry down a pail of warm water for you. I filled the tea-kettle just before I went down to get the mail."

Mamma Young moved rollingly away, patting her apron pocket that held the precious letters, and Phyllis turned back to her sweeping. She wanted to get the paper swept up and her letter read before Mamma Young came back with the pail of water.

She was reading the close, even script of her father's letter, which read so much like his other letters, when a shadow fell across her and she looked up to see Edna standing in the path waiting for her to move out of the doorway. She had brought the pail of hot water and soap and rags for the washing.

"Oh, thanks," Phyllis said, ashamed as a child to be caught reading a letter instead of working. She got to her feet and took the pail. The steam rose in her face. The water must be hot enough for scalding chickens, she thought. She would have to carry water from the house or the pump to cool it, or wait for it to cool. She wondered if Edna would say anything about her papering. Certainly she was not going to ask her how she liked it. "Um, you smell of apple butter!" she said pleasantly.

Edna was looking straight ahead of her into the little house. "Well, it's a wonder I don't smell of *rotten* apples," she said, "with the kind of bushelful the boys brought in for me to cut up and use the best I could. I hope we can afford to spray with some decent sort of spray next year. That stuff Ralph got sure wasn't much use. Good half the apples wormy!"

"It was all right where they *used* it!" Phyllis said, hotly. "The trees they sprayed with that Ralph got were all right." Edna shrugged her shoulders as though to say: "A lot you know about it," and turned away. Phyllis watched her walking heavily toward the house. She looked like a worn, middle-aged woman. Phyllis remembered she *had* brought the water for her and wanted to call after her to thank her again, but her throat closed on the words. Perhaps not kindness but curiosity had prompted her coming. Let her go her bitter way!

Phyllis turned back to her work. The papering did look handsome. The panels between the rows of brownish, rough oatmeal paper were not all of the same pattern, but were of pieces that went together nicely, and they were very evenly cut and pasted. She had been proud of her work, but the pride and joy of doing that had sustained her through three days of very hard work was gone, suddenly, since Edna's visit. She felt sad, and very tired. She wished for her father and his calm, appraising belief in her. Ralph, when he came in from the orchard at noon, would see the finished work and be pleased and very proud. She tried to imagine just what he would say. Was she always, her life long, her marriage long, to feel the hunger she felt for him to be glad in her and in whatever she did? She stooped to pick up a broomstraw from the floor and moved to the window. The panes were dirty with many months of living-dirt left by the renters, the dust of moving, and daubs of papering paste. The sun that came through made shafts of mote-swirling light that slanted to the floor. With the straw-end she idly drew on the pane a penmanship dove, the kind her father had taught her to make when she was a little girl. A wave of longing and love for her husband came over her and she began to write him a letter. "Darling," she wrote rapidly, "in the morning you are always away from me and I think it a pity. Why must work always take you away from me in the morning? Here is this sun and here am I. And I love you so. I think I love you most of all in the middle of the morning. This once, leave the work and come up. Leave the orchard and come up to our house."

There was the sound of hurrying feet on the path. Phyllis stooped quickly, caught up the rag Edna had brought, plunged it into the hot water, and wiped it across the pane, washing away the letter. She dropped the rag onto the window-sill and turned to meet whoever had come. It was her little daughter.

"What are you doing, Mother?" Betty asked. "Did *you* draw that bird?"

"Yes," Phyllis said, and wiped her hands on her apron. "Did Mamma Young send you?"

Betty came close and looked at the bird, her head on one side, her hands clasped behind her. "What were you *doing*, Mother?" she asked.

"What makes you think I was doing anything?" Phyllis laughed.

"I saw you wash it off. Was it another bird? It looked like writing."

Phyllis leaned against the window. "Did Mamma Young curl your hair?" she asked. "I neglect you. When we get moved in I'll really look after you. We'll get caught up on your lessons. We'll learn a poem every day."

"Were you *writing* a poem?" Betty lifted her mother's arm and drew it about her shoulders and asked again: "Mother, what *were* you doing? If you don't tell me I can't stand it."

"I was writing a letter to Daddy," Phyllis said, as matter-of-factly as she could; "there!"

"Oh," Betty said, "then what made you look so naughty? I guess it *was* a poem!"

Phyllis was troubled that Betty should think it naughty to write a poem, but she was at a loss to think of anything to say about it. The child seemed to sense her embarrassment. "Oh," she said, remembering, "Gran'ma says for you to come up and feed the baby. And old Gran'ma keeps saying: 'Whose child is that crying? Whose child is that crying?'" Betty puckered her lips and squinted her eyes in what she thought was a very old look.

"Why, Betty, you monkey, I'm ashamed of you!" Phyllis said. "Come on. We'll go look after the baby."

They walked up the path, swinging hands. "She knows, all right, whose child it is," Betty said. "She just talks that way. She *pretends*." Then: "But you couldn't *send* the letter, Mother."

"It wasn't written to be sent. I just wrote it."

"I'll race you, Mother. One for the money; two for the show!"

"That child's been howling his head off," old

199

Grandma greeted Phyllis. "He's been crying for hours."

"No, he hasn't," Mamma Young said patiently. "He woke up only awhile ago, but it is time to feed him."

"Mamie, you're the most impudent child I've raised, the way you contradict! If it weren't for the shame of it, big as you are, I'd give you a slap."

Mamma Young laughed.

Phyllis took her baby up from the bed in the kitchen corner and sat down in the little rocker to nurse him.

Old Grandma came to her, put her hand on her shoulder, and said: "You aren't the young woman's got my room now, are you?"

"No," Phyllis said, "and it's your room now, Gran'ma. You've your own room, your own bed again."

"Yes, that's right, I recall now. Mamie moved me back in there, didn't she? Mamie! Mamie, I don't know as it's a good thing to be moving me round the way you do, at my age, out of one bed and into another. I caught a chill when you moved me last and I ain't been able to throw it off. All this moving! You never seem to settle down and make up your mind how you want things. When we built this

200

house we had it all settled, how everything was to be, and then you wanted it different, you and that girl, what's her name—Jenny. Don't I recall there was some *reason* I was to sleep out here in the kitchen? Am I discommoding? Am I putting somebody out, being back in my own bed again?"

"You're all right, Gran'ma," Mamma Young said again, in all patience. "You're to sleep in your own bed right along now."

"Well, then, who's in my bed in there now? I come back there after breakfast and there's a woman in my bed, a stranger. And she was in there last time I went in the room. And I didn't just fancy it, either. You think I fancy things, Mamie, and say I do, to put me off and get round me, and I *don't*. She's there, in my bed."

"Will you stir this butter," Edna asked Mamma Young, "and not let it scorch while I go down and bring up some more jars?" Edna and Phyllis had paid no attention to each other.

"I think I'll take the baby upstairs to nurse him," Phyllis said, weary, almost to tears, of work and talk and Young women.

"Well, you can nurse him in my room, if you've a mind to," Grandma Young offered, "and not climb those stairs. But I can't *get in* my room. The door's locked. The door's to, and locked fast, and I can't budge it. Somebody's in there, taking my bed to pieces, sounds like."

"Cleo's in there," Little Betty said. "She had a letter, an airmail, special-delivery letter, Gran'ma said it was. I took it in to Cleo, when Gran'ma brought the mail in, and Cleo sat up in bed and said: 'Good God!'"

"Here, here, here!" old Grandma said, and trotted her feet on the floor. "Whose child are you, talking like that? Don't you know that's the Lord's name in vain? Come here! Mamie, is this child yours, talking so? If you were mine I'd scour your mouth. I'd wash your mouth out with soap for you to remember by. My! Did you hear what she said, Mamie?"

"Do you suppose she got bad news?" Mamma Young asked Phyllis. "She's not been outa that room all morning. You don't suppose there's anything wrong. You don't think we should call her, ask if she's all right?"

Edna had come up from the cellar, her apron full of glass jars. "She's not wrung her own neck," she said. "Gone back to sleep, likely."

"Gran'ma, may I please have some bread and hot apple butter?" Betty asked Mamma Young. "It smells *so* good!"

Phyllis could not help smiling at Betty's very grown-up "It smells so good," but she felt vexed with the child too. Why couldn't she be a natural little girl without such canny, woman's ways? Edna would be annoyed at Betty's asking for a piece in the middle of the morning. Keeping the child home from school, to be taught by her own mother, Edna, and all the Youngs, for that matter, thought pure foolishness.

Phyllis got up and started for the stair door, wanting to be out of hearing before Edna could say anything.

"Just a minute and I'll fix you a slice, Lamb," Mamma Young was saying. "Wait till I finish peeling this apple."

Upstairs in her own room, Phyllis thought about her new house while she lay nursing her baby. She should be able to get the woodwork, windows, and floor cleaned that afternoon, and perhaps in the morning the menfolks would carry out the heavier pieces of furniture for her. She was to have the bed and dresser from the ell room and a chair here and a table there from other rooms. She and Ralph and Betty would go on having their meals with the family. At least their evenings and their nights they would spend in their own home.

She remembered the letter she had written to Ralph in the dust of the window-pane. The letter itself and her having written it were both now like a dream. "You've a funny ma!" she said to her son, and brushed his hair with her palm. "And you're getting to be an awful load to carry up and down stairs. Tomorrow you'll be in your own house. Like that? Yes, tomorrow." She moved him to her other side, and a sharp pain shot across her shoulders. She was terribly tired from the papering. She closed her eyes and saw clearly, for an instant, a green hill with the covered wagon of Wallpaper Abbie atop it.

There was somebody coming upstairs. Phyllis felt a little anger, in her tiredness, at not being left alone to rest. How could Mamma Young go on, never resting in the day time unless she was really "down sick," never knowing any escape from old Grandma and Edna and the everlasting hard work, except the escape she found in a hymn sung to herself.

It was Cleo who had come up. She rapped with her nails on the door and came in and over to the bed. She was dressed in her only good dress, a gray crepe with violet cuffs and a tied scarf. Phyllis thought she had never seen her looking so pretty.

"Did Mrs. Young get a letter from Harve this

morning?" she asked at once.

"It was for Grandpa Young," Phyllis said. "She didn't read it."

Cleo sat down in a little rocking-chair. "I don't care about that," she said. "Was there anything in it? Did he send a check?"

"Yes, there was a check for Grandpa."

"How much?"

"Forty-five."

"Nothing for me?"

"I don't think so."

"Well, now, isn't that cute! You'd think he could send his check to me just once. He's told the old man to hand me a ten or five, like he did the last time, I bet!"

Phyllis did not say anything. Like Mamma Young, she felt that Harvey had done well to send so much.

"Doesn't he think I *need* anything?" Cleo said. "This is the only dress I've got to my name, this old thing!"

"You look lovely in it," Phyllis said.

"Well, I'll *tell* you something! I'm packed. To-night I'm getting out, and I suppose there'd better be someone know it, so they won't think I'm kid-napped and get the police or sheriff, or whatever they've got here, out after me and be wiring Harve. Keep it under your hat, will you, until I'm gone awhile? I've stuck round here as long as I can stand it. If Harve had treated me half decent I'd have stayed by him, but he hasn't. You know how he was when he was here, and now what does he do? Can't even write! Sends his check to his dad, and I can have a five or a ten out of it, like a kid! I'm getting out tonight, and nothing'll stop me this time."

"How are you going? Who are you going with, Cleo?"

"That's all right, who I'm going with. He'll see, Harve'll see! There's some men that can hold their job and hang onto enough to treat a person right with, even now. And if these Youngs think I'm the only girl Harve ever had or that he's the only man I can have they're crazy. I gave up plenty for Harve Young and I'm through."

She laughed her high, brittle laugh, and went on: "You know last Christmas when I wanted to get Harve something and hadn't a cent? Well, I wrote a girl, used to have an apartment next to me, and asked her if she could let me have a ten, and the night of the day she got my letter she went to a party, and this man I used to know was there, and she told him about hearing from me and that she

206

didn't have the ten to send and he said he could let her have it. I'd known him a lot longer'n I had Harve. I gave him up for Harve, if you want to know, and I was a fool to do it. When Harve got his job and sent the first check, I sent her five of the ten I owed her—thought I owed her—and she wrote then who I had to thank, and I wrote him, and I've heard from him a couple of times, and he wants to get me out of this; he's all right, Fred is."

"What about Harvey?" Phyllis asked. "You'll write him, won't you? If you're going with someone else, like this, you'll set him free, won't you?"

"He'll be free enough, don't you worry! Harve's not just the darling boy his folks think he is. He'll be free enough to keep on persuading himself he don't want this and he don't like that! All you know is Harve reading a book out loud after supper. His whole family—" Cleo groped in first one pocket and then the other for cigarettes. "I was crazy about Harve," she sobbed, suddenly, the lighted cigarette between her thin, trembling lips. "I took everything from him, everything! I gave up everybody and everything! I spent like a fool, bought things I couldn't pay for, that he never even noticed I had on. And twice I worked it so he could hold his job there. He wasn't half doing his work when he was rushing that Doris girl who let him down, and one of the boys tipped me off that they were going to let him go if he didn't snap out of it, and I got after him, kept at him, did a good half of his work myself, until he was taking hold again. And do you think he ever thanked me for it? Not on your life! Thought I was lucky to have him back, I guess, at any price!" She went to the dresser to get a match and stood looking at her reflection through half-shut eyes. "And his folks are so sure I've ruined his sweet life! Even Tom!"

"Write to Harvey," Phyllis said again. "Get a divorce, Cleo, and marry—"

"Marry? I've *been* married. Once is enough! Harve can have a divorce if he wants it. I like Fred. We got on and we will again. And, take it from me, I'd rather be with a man I can get on with and am not nuts about!"

She took a silver compact from her pocket and tossed it onto the bed. "That's for Betty," she said. "Wish I could get her something. She's a mighty cute kid!" She whirled and went out quickly and Phyllis heard the sound of her heels on the stairs.

The baby, awake again, fed and happy, reached for the compact with both hands, and Phyllis, surprised at the strength of his grasp, let him hold it.

208

There was the sound of much hurrying down-stairs. The kitchen screen-door squeaked to several times. Tom's voice rose excitedly. Surely it was not time for the men to come in for dinner. Perhaps Tom had come up to look for something they needed in their work. Tom had a way of turning the house over and making all the women feel at fault when he could not find something he wanted.

She must go down and help with the dinner. She dreaded lifting the baby again. He was growing so heavy, and her back was so tired from the papering. Maybe it would be well to take another day about washing the woodwork and windows. But she wanted the work done, wanted very much to be in her own home. Poor Jenny! If Cousin Jim's job failed, as it very likely might, they would be coming, the four of them, to make their home in the house. She would so much rather see Jenny taking over the ell room that had been hers so long, than Edna's boys. What a time she had had persuading Ralph to let her keep Betty home from school for a year, to teach the child herself! Even Mamma Young had been against her. She could not come out and say simply that she was determined to have the child free from Edna's boys' teasing and meannesses. Already Betty was less nervous, less likely to start crying at the least little thing, but she was getting to be such a grown-up, such a little actress of a grown-up. In a day or two, the moving done, she felt she could give enough time to the child to justify herself in keeping her at home.

The thought of Cleo saddened her. How little they, any of them, had come to know her, for all her months in the house!

The unusual noises downstairs went on. A horse galloped up to the house and away again. Phyllis got up, lifted the baby, and went to the stairs. Her mother-in-law was coming up. "Oh, Phyllis, girl," she panted, "I was coming up to tell you!"

"Ralph?" Phyllis cried. "Has something happened to Ralph? Betty?"

"No. No, it's Edna. Ralph's gone to Ferguson's to phone the doctor, gone on old Bill. Arch *told* the boys not to take the car to pieces again! She's in my room. Tom and Arch carried her in from the little house. I don't know how bad she's hurt. It's her back, mostly, I think."

Mamma Young turned on the stairs and went tremblingly down, ahead of Phyllis. "We were washing the woodwork. Edna was doing the window-casings. I'm no good at climbing. That table you've used for all your papering gave way and let her down. Here I thought I'd say at dinner: 'The house is ready and you boys can take the time to carry the pieces out for Phyllis, so she can get settled.' You've worked so hard. Poor Edna! She's suffering so."

Edna lay on Mamma Young's bed under a quilt. Tom stood at the foot of the bed, his hands clamped

around the posts. Old Grandma was hovering near, rubbing her wrists and talking to herself. Cleo stood by the window twisting her handkerchief. She looked at Phyllis, wide-eyed, resentfully helpless.

Edna's face was gray and twisted with pain. When she saw Phyllis she gave her short, breathy laugh, started to say something, and then closed her mouth tightly.

Grandpa Young came from the kitchen. "I've got a good fire going, Mamie," he said. "Don't you suppose you oughta fix a hot pack or something? Maybe heat would stop the pain a little. Don't *you* think a hot pack, Ma?"

Old Grandma coughed, pleased to be asked her opinion, and said: "It surely couldn't hurt any. I don't know yet what 'tis that's happened. Did you fall pickin' apples, Edna?"

"Leave me alone!" Edna said. "Leave me be!" Sweat stood out on her face. She had folded her arms tightly under the quilt.

"Gosh!" Cleo said over by the window, "can't you *do* something?"

Little Betty had come in and was standing by her grandmother, holding to her apron. "Daddy's gone to phone the doctor," she said. She looked a very much frightened, sympathetic little girl, with none of the acting nonsense about her, and Phyllis felt a warm, mother-feeling toward her.

Edna moaned and turned her head from side to side, against her shoulders.

Grandpa, troubled, and not knowing what to do, whistled a little through his teeth. The baby, in Phyllis's arms, gave a lurch and a squeal of pleasure and let fly the compact he had carried downstairs fast in his two hands. It hit the floor with a noise that was startling in the quiet room, and rolled under the bed. Betty got down on hands and knees to go after it, but Phyllis said sharply: "Let it alone now!"

"Can't I do something, Edna?" Mamma Young asked. "Can't I fix the hot cloths and see if they won't help some?"

"You can pack the boys' clothes, if you will," Edna said. "You'll have to iron their shirts, and some need mending. I want them to go stay with my brothers while I'm laid up." She stopped and her face twisted again in pain. "I want them to go today."

"Why, Child dear, we'll take care of your boys," Mamma Young said. "I'll put up their lunches and see to their clothes. You're not to worry. The doctor'll come soon." She put out patting hands that did not quite touch Edna's shoulder.

"That's right," Tom said hoarsely, "we'll look after the boys."

Edna raised her head a little from the pillow, caught her breath sharply, and said: "You do what I *say*, Tom. I want the boys to go over there, and if this should be something I'd not get over, I want them to *have* the boys, all three!"

"Why, Edna, you're sick," Tom said. "You don't realize what you're saying. You're hurt bad, but you're going to get over it all right. We'll take care of the boys here." His voice was deep but unshaken.

"They're to go!" Edna said.

"They're my boys too," Tom said. "I'll take care of them."

"I want them to go," Edna said again. "I get my way in this. *You* take care of them! Mamma'll take care of them, that's who will. You'll not know they're around unless they get in your way!"

"I'll take care of them," Tom repeated.

Cleo had been holding to the window curtains, looking out. Now she turned. "Well, for God's sake," she cried at Tom, "leave her alone, can't you! Let her have what she *wants*, can't you? Treat her like a dog, let her work her head off! Now she's

214

down, let her have what she wants, can't you?"

Edna lifted her head and looked at Cleo. "What's it to you?" she cried. "What's this to you? I've never seen you lift a hand to lighten work for anyone! You'd have *taken* Tom and never blinked an eye, if you coulda got him! You keep outa this!"

"That's a lie," Cleo said. She went out, turning in the door to say: "You're right. It's nothing to me. Let him take or leave your kids!"

"Oh, dear," Mamma Young said, and wrapped her apron around Betty's shoulders as though to protect the child from all she was hearing and seeing.

"Don't fret, Edna," Grandpa Young said. "If you want your boys over to your brothers' for now, they're to go, acourse, and I'll take 'em over. Mamma'll get their clothes together and I'll go by school and take 'em over there. Tom'll go into the hospital with you, if the doctor says you have to go there, and stay as long as you need him. You're not to fret." He spoke gently, but as the one in authority.

"Why don't you go eat your dinner?" Edna asked. "It's in the oven and it'll be dried out. Can't somebody take up the dinner?"

"I'll take it up," said Phyllis.

"And I'll stay with you," Mamma Young comforted Edna, "and don't you think you could stand to have me put some liniment on your back? I'd be so careful. The doctor'll be here soon, if Ralph can locate him, and you know how he drives."

Tom paid no attention when Phyllis came into the bedroom to tell him that dinner was on the table.

"Go on, Son. Go and eat," Mamma Young urged. "There's nothing you can do."

Tom lingered, waiting for Edna to say again for him to go or stay. She said nothing and lay with her eyes closed.

They were a silent four at the table, Tom and his father, old Grandma and little Betty. Cleo stayed in old Grandma's room and Phyllis thought it as well not to call her. Little Betty remembered that her grandmother had said there was a letter from Uncle Harvey and got down from the table and ran to Mamma Young to get it herself for her grandfather. The old man read it and smiled to himself before he handed it over to Tom. "He's a good boy," he said fondly, "Harvey's a good boy, and he seems to like it down there, and the work. That's a lot to send home, and in a new place." Tom nodded his agreement.

The baby fretted, and Phyllis took him up from the bed in the kitchen corner and rocked him in the little rocker to quiet him.

"I should've seen to that table," Grandpa Young reproached himself. "I didn't know it was rickety. I didn't even know you were using it to stand on while you papered. It's a wonder it didn't let you down, Phyllis. You should have had one of the ladders instead. The boys and I should have helped you."

"I wanted to do it," Phyllis said.

The men were still at the table when the doctor came. The baby started crying anew when he heard the unfamiliar voice, and Phyllis carried him outside and walked up and down the path until he was quiet. Then she sat down on the running-board of the doctor's car to wait. There Ralph found her when he rode into the yard on old Bill.

"The ambulance will be here directly," he told her. "The doctor said, when I talked with him on the phone, he thought we'd better bring her in to the hospital for an X-ray. I seem a good while getting back? I ran old Bill pretty hard going over; thought I'd better let him walk, coming back. He's no race-horse. What does Doc say now?"

"I don't know. I've been out here with the baby. He was crying. There's been disturbance enough. Tom and Edna were quarreling and Cleo took Edna's part against Tom."

"Quarreling! *Now?* What's the matter with him, anyhow?"

"You're hot and sweaty as old Bill. You'll not be sick, Ralph, riding like that? Go in and get Betty, will you? She's in the house somewhere, all eyes. She remembers *everything*."

"She'll be all right," Ralph said, and leaned against the car, his elbow in the window, his foot on the running-board. "It's the hospital," he said. "I bet it's that, much as anything, upset Tom. She'll have to go, of course, and stay as long as she needs to, but I don't know how we'll handle it, Baby. Doc'll wait, like he's still waiting for half our bill, but the hospital— How much is it a day, do you know?"

"Harvey sent a check for forty-five."

"He did? That's fine! Guess this's the ambulance coming."

In the afternoon Mamma Young and Phyllis had the kitchen to themselves, for old Grandma had chosen to rest on the folding couch in the dining-room for once, and Cleo was still in old Grandma's bedroom.

Phyllis ironed shirts for Edna's boys while Mamma Young mended and sewed on buttons.

"Well, it certainly was the last thing I expected to see—Edna to faint away like that when they lifted

218

her to carry her. For an instant I thought she was gone, yes, I did. I think we all thought it, all but the doctor—Tom most of all. Edna's been so strong always and ready to stand anything. To see her faint away! Tom was scared, I tell you, and no wonder. I never saw him so. He called her by name, started in on the doctor to make him do something for her, and calling on me to help.

"Oh, Phyllis, I've been so concerned to see things go the way they have for them, so long. I've seen it before in other people. 'Twas that way with Arch's brother Joe and his wife; just driving hard every day to get the work done and get ahead and never anything else, and Tom's not a grasping man, not that hard-driving a man by nature. People've got to be of one mind in more than just that they're *going to get up early* and get the work done, or life's not good. Work's all right and you have to do it, but it's not enough. It's like the proverb: 'Better's a dinner of herbs where love is than a stalled ox and hatred.' I wouldn't say they've downright hated, but there's been a widening between them that it's been hard to see go on. I don't know whether it's something they can pull out of now or not, but I wish it for them so. If Tom could just stay feeling like he was while Edna was in that faint—not that scared—I'd not wish that for him, but that *mindful* of Edna!"

"Was it Edna's idea to wash the woodwork in the little house?"

"No. No, I thought of it and said I was going to see if I could get it done before the menfolk came in for dinner, and she said she'd help, since we were having baked hash, and it already in the oven. I think it's not been easy for her to bear, you and Ralph having a house to move into, even that little old one that you've had to work on so to make over. I think it's been hard for her to see you fixing it up, and her staying on here. The place you gave up is away, and theirs is right across the road where she can't help but see and think of it every day. She set so much by that house. It meant more to her than any house'll ever have to mean to you, Phyllis. You can't blame her her grudging, much. Things are hard for her and it don't lighten trouble, when it comes up, to know it's a good part your own fault."

Mamma Young sighed after such a long speech. "Even Cleo," she added, "though she took a strange way to show it, sees things are hard for Edna—too hard. It was strange, Cleo turning on Tom like that, wasn't it, taking Edna's part? I think she's felt it that not since the day Harvey left and she was so ugly to him has Tom taken her part any, even once. Family feeling is awful strong in a man like Tom, but it's true what Edna said, he's never had the concern for his boys you'd expect of him. They're so much more Edna's and her folks', in looks and everything, than they are his—ours. He's never made the fuss over them Arch made over his, but they're his boys, and I think, brought home to him like it was, at a time like this, he'll feel it, show it more. Goodness knows he's worked hard enough for them."

Little Betty had gone with her father and grandfather to the orchard.

"I hated it so," Phyllis said, when she was folding the last little shirt, "to have Betty hear all that talk. What could she think? She doesn't forget anything."

"I know," Mamma Young said, "and it's true, what Arch said that time when he'd stood all he could of the way things were going, we've never had contention, ever. Arch had Quakers on his father's side the house, and maybe that accounts. We got on, Arch and me, from the beginning, and I was bound, when old Gran'ma came to live with us, nothing was to spoil it, and I never bickered with her. The boys growing up not to know strife in the house has made it extra hard for them now, I think.

Edna's folks, all of them, have a kinda rough, gruff way about them and I think that, in Edna, didn't set well with Tom. He used to be just quiet, not cross. He was never short-spoken at home, like he is now. The boys played together so well when they were small, Tom and Ralph, though Tom was older, and Harvey was the best-natured little fellow. The other boys, and Arch, just couldn't do enough for him. It's the times we've had, I guess.

"That was a relief to Arch, that forty-five coming from Harvey today. Part of it he'll give Cleo, I suppose. He didn't hand me over the letter, so I don't know, but I suppose he'll share it with her. I declare, I'd think that girl would wear out from pure lone-liness, staying cooped up in there all the time. I saved dinner for her. You'd think she'd get hungry by and by."

When Mamma Young called to let the menfolks know it was time for Grandpa to go to the school-house for Edna's boys, Betty came up to the house with the men.

"Had a time keepin' this young'un from climbing trees," Grandpa said. "One to fall and get hurt's enough for a day. Can she go along with me, Mamie, to take the boys over?"

"I don't see why not," Mamma Young said. "Get

222

your hat, Pet, and your sweater too. It may be cold by the time you come home." Phyllis would have liked the child to stay home, but she was too tired, and too anxious to have everything go smoothly for the rest of the day, to protest, and Betty ran to old Grandma's room, where her wraps were kept in the big wardrobe, to get her hat and sweater.

"Cleo is writing a letter, Mother," she said when she came back to the kitchen. She reached up, put her arm about her mother's neck, and drew her down to whisper: "Cleo said I could *have* that powder-box of hers that rolled under Gran'ma's bed. I didn't *ask* for it."

"Did you thank her?"

"I *think* I did. I went in *alone* and got it from under the bed. Can I take it, may I take it along, in the wagon?" She patted her sweater pocket that held the precious compact.

"Don't make it *bad* to the little boys, now, Arch," Mamma Young admonished. "Just tell them she fell and hurt herself. 'Torn ligaments' sounds so painful. And the doctor says he's pretty certain there's no bones broken. I expect she'll be home in a few days."

"I'll go by Ferguson's, coming home, and phone in and find out how she is," Grandpa said. "I told Tom to stay in if Edna wants him there. She may want him to stay until she's easier. Now don't destroy the paper, Mamie. I scarcely got a chance to look at it this noon. Put it up for me. I want to read it."

"Is there anything special?" Mamma Young asked in alarm. "Not floods or anything, Arch?"

"Nope, just news. All Europe and Africa apoppin', looks like, that's all." He whistled a little. "You read the papers and you think civilization won't last till Christmas."

"What's civilization?" little Betty asked.

"There's a corker for you, Son. I can't tell you, Pet. Something to fight for, seems like, mostly. Ask your dad there."

Old Grandma came tottering out of the dining-room carrying the baby in her arms.

"Why, Gran'ma, you're not to take the baby up, and you know it!" Mamma Young cried, and hurried to take the baby from her.

"Well, I'd like to know why not! I'm not going to leave a baby lie and fret. Spent half my life carry'n' 'em, I guess. And when they wasn't mine they were yours, Mamie."

"That's right, Gran'ma," Ralph said, "but you've about served your time, don't you think? You better leave him in his basket for Mamma and Phyllis to look after. Can't have you dropping him. That's *my* boy, you know that?"

"Yes, sir, it looks like war, that's what it looks like," Grandpa said, "and the other side's a lot closer than it once was. If that turns out a real war it's a question how long before we'll be drug into it ourselves."

"He's a fine baby, and he'll make a fine man, if you can raise him," old Grandma went on. "Arch, don't you talk about wars! I've had enough of that. Seen enough. Seems like it's the first thing I remember, war talk. Silas and I, we'd stand and listen to my Uncle Hadley (my great-uncle that was, and he had only one leg) talk and tell war stories. This is a fine boy, Son, if you can raise him."

"That's it," Ralph said solemnly, seeing, through the tenderness he felt for his old grandmother, a sobering importance in her words that none of the others would see. "Do the best I can, Gran'ma, but I don't seem to be making a very good start for 'em."

"How many you got? These two? That's not much, and you're young. My, you don't seem but a boy to me, and nowheres near old enough to shoulder lookin' after a family!"

Ralph sighed. "Likely I've no business to have them," he said.

"Here, here!" his mother cried, and swung the baby high. He waved his arms, kicked hard, and laughed out, loudly. "What a way to talk! Well, he feels he's got business to *be*. I never saw a stronger, finer boy for his age, and I've had some pretty fine boys myself."

Ralph went out with his father to put the team to the wagon and carried the suitcase full of clothes for Edna's boys.

"That old suitcase is the one Ralph used first year he went down to school." Mamma Young said. "Now, don't you mind that talk!" she comforted. "They're just low, seeing someone hurt so bad, and this hospital business ahead, and all. Men have to talk that way, it seems. I'll put the baby down and we'll hope he'll stay good until feeding time. And, Gran'ma, you're not to *touch* him, understand?"

"Just as you say," old Grandma pouted. "Ive seen the time you were glad enough to let me mind 'em. I'm going in and sit and watch him. I'm not going to leave him lie and fret."

From the kitchen window Phyllis watched Ralph swing Betty up onto the high wagon-seat beside Grandpa, raise his hand in good-by, turn, and walk slowly toward the house. She must be good to him, she told herself. She must be comforting, far-sighted,

226

and cheerful and somehow lighten the burden that was on him.

Ralph came in, got himself a drink, and stood looking at her, the glass in his hand. "My, you look domestic, Baby," he said. "What you going to do with all that flour?"

Bantering from him, when she had steeled herself for gloom, surprised Phyllis, disarmed her.

"Something has to be done with all these apples Mother peeled," she said coolly. "I thought I'd make some pies."

"Can't they wait? I came back to see if you wouldn't come down to the orchard with me—sit and watch me sort apples."

"Sit and *watch* you?"

"That's right. And talk to me. Tell me what's on your mind."

"*On my mind?*"

"That's what I said."

"There's nothing on my mind." Her voice was trembling.

"Well, what you so cross about, then?"

"Cross?" Phyllis cried. "I'm *not* cross! How can you *say* that? You come in here—say you wish you didn't have a family, let old Gran'ma say we'll never raise the boy!" All her tired, pent-up feeling came in a rush of sobbing words and she was astonished, herself, at them. "Grandpa talking war, Edna hurt and in the hospital! We've been *weeks* getting the house fixed and we're not moved and you don't care if we're not! And you haven't *looked* at my wall-paper!" Tears were streaming down her cheeks. She wiped them away with the back of her floury hand. "And I'm so sorry for Cleo, and for Jenny," she sobbed aloud. "I don't *understand* Betty, and I'm so tired—I can't stand it!"

"Well, forever more!" Ralph said slowly, set the glass down in the sink, and came and put his arms around her and held her head against him. "Don't cry," he soothed. "We'll get you moved tomorrow, before breakfast if you say so. I did, I did look at the paper, and I think it's swell. Don't cry; leave this stuff and come on down to the orchard with me."

Phyllis cried on, ashamed, but glad beyond measure of the comfort of his arms. "I can't," she said at last. "I can't go off and leave pies. Mother'd finish them and she's done too much now. Anyway, I—I've got to feed the baby pretty soon, if we're going to *raise* him." She laughed through her crying and he laughed with her a little and held her head against him and stroked her hair.

"You won't go with me?"

"I can't."

"Okay then." Still holding her, swaying her gently from side to side, he began to sing to her, a song that must have belonged to his childhood, that she had never heard before:

"The last time I did spy-ah
She was makin' apple pie-ah
And my heart for her did sigh-ah
'Way down on the Bingo farm."

He held her at arm's length and sang on:

"I asked her did she love me.
She said she was above me,
And out the door she shoved me,
'Way down on the Bingo farm!"

He kissed her on the neck and went away, down toward the orchard, singing loudly:

"I ain't goin' there any more,
I ain't goin' there any more,
I ain't goin' there any more,
'Way down on the Bingo farm!"

Phyllis washed her face, dried it on the roller towel, and went back to her pie-making, strangely rested, comforted. She remembered that in the outpouring of her griefs she had not mentioned the greatest of them all, their concern about their living, and her father's plight.

Mamma Young came in and old Grandma with her, when Phyllis was taking the pies from the oven.

"That's a fine-looking pie," old Grandma said. "Looks nice and light-crusted. Who taught you to bake, Girl?"

"I taught myself," Phyllis said, "from a book, and for a while I had a girl to help me who made wonderful pies. Olga, her name was."

"I don't recall her," old Grandma said. "But did you bake the edge trimmings? I always did, and you too, don't you, Mamie? Don't you bake them for the children?"

Phyllis brought the pan of trimmings for old Grandma to sample, and she smacked her lips over them and pronounced them "good as they looked."

Phyllis decided to set the table in the dining-room. There were to be so few of them for supper, only seven, and she would not need to widen the table. Petunias from Mamma Young's flower-bed, in a blue cream-pitcher on one of Phyllis's gay table-covers, made the supper-table quite festive for such a sober day.

"Do you think," Phyllis asked Mamma Young,

"they'll think it too bright?"

"Oh, I don't think so," Mamma Young considered; "there won't be but Arch and Ralph and I don't think they'll think anything but that it's nice. They'll be hungry too. I must pick a good bouquet and send it in to the hospital with whoever goes in tomorrow. Ralph'll have to get the car back together now, and running."

Supper had to wait while Ralph did the chores alone. Grandpa Young was late getting home too. Betty was very tired from the long ride and staggered into the house sleepily.

"We had to wait a while over at Ferguson's before we could get the line," Grandpa told them, "and then it was a while before I could find out anything. There's no bones broken, but Doc thinks she'd better not be moved for a few days. Tom'll be out early in the morning—come out with the Hartleys when they come from taking the milk. Mrs. Hartley was on the line, to hear how Edna was, and she said they'd go round by the hospital for Tom. I told the nurse I talked with to tell him. Supper in the dining-room, Mamie? Well, I'm hungry and so's this young'un, if she can keep awake long enough to eat."

Betty revived when she saw the gay table, and

231

wanted to sit by her grandfather. The child took turns pledging life companionship to first one of her grandparents and then the other, and this day she had been her grandpa's girl. She was much awed to hear her Aunt Edna's name mentioned in the blessing, and peeked at her grandfather over clasped hands, in wonder.

"Well, I'm thankful it's no worse than it is," Mamma Young said, "though a sprain can be bad and bother a long time. When the pain lets up I think Edna should be glad of a few days in bed. She needs the rest."

"Edna's brothers have *five* dogs, and a gun apiece and fishing-poles and boots hung up in the *kitchen*," Betty told them, and the *men* peel the potatoes and get supper all alone!"

"The boys'll be all right there," Grandpa assured them. "There's a school just a mile from the place, and they won't need to miss a day."

Cleo had come out when called to supper. There was color in her face, and her eyes were very bright. Phyllis saw that both Grandpa and Ralph noticed her prettiness and that she was wearing her good dress.

"There's a check in Harve's letter that came today," Grandpa told Cleo kindly. "He wants you

232

to have some of it." He took his wallet from his hip pocket and counted three five-dollar bills and handed them across the table to her. Cleo thanked him, without smiling, and put the bills in her pocket. After supper she astonished them all by helping Phyllis carry out the dishes.

"Phyllis, you ought to see the orchard. There's a moon," Ralph said. "You can come now, can't you?"

"Yes, you go on and get outside a little," Mamma Young urged. "I'll get old Gran'ma and the children to bed. Betty's half asleep now."

"No, I'm not," said Betty. "I'm all awake now. I want to go too. Are you going to show Daddy the bird, Mother?"

"What bird, Sleepyhead?" Ralph asked, and picked her up in his arms. "You're dreaming already."

"I'm not dreaming. The bird on the window over where Mother washed the letter away."

"You're clear cuckoo," Ralph said. "Want Daddy to carry you upstairs?"

With both hands she waved kisses to her grandparents, Cleo, and old Grandma and nestled her head in her father's neck. "It was a letter and a bird," she insisted sleepily before her eyes closed.

Mamma Young hustled old Grandma off to her room to get her to bed. Grandpa went outside and the two young women were left alone. Cleo asked: "Do you think Harve said I was to have fifteen?"

"I don't know," Phyllis said, "I expect so. He'd have sent more if he could, I'm sure."

"Yes, I guess he would," Cleo said. "He's all right, Harve is. You forget what I said this morning. He's all right—if only—" She moved to the open door and stood, her arms folded, her head thrown back against the door-casing, looking out. "I'd have stayed if he wanted me, if he'd half wanted me. He didn't. That's the truth! And I sure couldn't go on takin' what Edna takes, all my life!"

"I think—Mamma Young thinks—it's going to be better for her."

"Well, gosh, I hope so. Fred's come. He's driven by twice. I expect he's waiting up by the cotton-woods for it to get darker. I put my bag down by the front gate. I wrote to Harve. I'll mail it some-where tomorrow. You tell Harve's folks good-by for me. Better wait a while, though. And Tom." She glanced over her shoulder at the mantel clock. She gave Phyllis's arm a squeeze with her fingers and walked quickly through the house toward the little-used front porch.

234

"Good luck, Cleo!" Phyllis called softly after her, as Ralph opened the stair door.

"Come on, now," he said, "leave the dishes and come on. I'll wipe them for you when we get back. That poor kid was so sleepy. Asleep before I got her

upstairs. I took off her shoes and stockings and rolled her into bed. She's had a big day."

"We all have."

The evening was cool. Already the moon spread shadows over the walls of the little house and whitened the tall orchard grass. Cicadas sang in the quiet. They walked with their arms about each other, quiet too.

"How's the tiredness?" Ralph asked.

"It's lifting."

"Well, how do you like 'em? Left two trees for

you to see how they hang. Aren't they fine, though?"

"Lovely."

"Papa thinks it's going to be a hard winter—worse than last."

"Old Gran'ma says so too."

"Is your dress pink or yellow, Baby? I can't tell in the moonlight."

"My old pink one. Ralph, do you think Harvey is all right down there? Do you think he's happier?"

"Oh, I'd say so. He's got work, and he's got away. That's what he wanted. Sounded all right in his letter."

"Ralph, do you think it will be any better now, for Tom and Edna?"

"Don't know, Pet. I hope so."

"It *was* better when they put her in the ambulance, when she opened her eyes."

"Well, things change, acourse, and people."

"We don't!"

"That's right."

"Not in new places, not in hard winters, not ever!"

"That's right."

"Oh, Ralph, when I think, when I think—"

"Think you're walking in the orchard with your old man. That's what to think. This is the place I

236

picked out when I was a kid at home, last fall I was home. This is the place, I said, I'd bring my girl some day. I wish I could build here, Baby."

8/10/99:

An absolutely delightful book! Purchased @ Wall Drug in S.D. on 7.18.99. Feel like I've known some of these people -and well - in my lifetime. Shed a few tears, and had many a Chuckle, while reading.

Chuck Weidel